Praise for the Book

This is a delightfully mysterious read that includes the all too familiar characters within this series. While it isn't necessary to know them, it adds to the adventure to read about their new liaisons, shenanigans and ongoing relationships. As a member of Columbine Club who has ridden the Royal Gorge Express, I can only say I never have had an adventure like this one [but] I truly can think of a few [members] who would be up for this kind of adventure. I think all 24 of the Columbine ladies plus some former members are looking forward to reading it. This book is a keeper.

—Joanie Liebman, member of Custer County
Columbine Club

We finished the book and really like it. Lynette likes the name you used [Pennie]; she thought it fit perfectly. No critique from me. It was a fun read and I appreciate you letting us look at it early.

—Shannon Byerly, Custer County Sheriff

I LOVED working on this book. Courtney weaves in so many clever components, and he brings the characters alive. I'm ready to visit them at St. Jude's! This book promises to entertain you and includes laugh-out-loud parts, with some clever play on word parts "sprinkled in." He has created a masterpiece.

—P. A. Ireland, Editor

Other Books by Award-Winning Author Courtney Miller

**The First Raven Mocker, Book 1
of The Cherokee Chronicles**
   Beverly Hills Book Award
   International Book Award
   NIEA Excellence Award for Historical Fiction

**The Raven Mocker's Legacy,
Book 2 of The Cherokee Chronicles**
   Book Excellence Award for "Literary
   Excellence in Faction"

**Gihli, The Chief Named Dog,
Book 3 of The Cherokee Chronicles**
   CAL Literary Novel Award
   Extravaganza Draft to Dream Book
   Competition Finalist

**Ludwig's Fugue,
Book 1 of The White Feather Mysteries**
   Rated "Outstanding" in all categories by
   Reader's Digest

**It's About Time,
Book 2 of The White Feather Mysteries**
   Extravaganza Draft to Dream Book
   Competition Winner

**Ghosts of St. Jude
(New for 2020)**

COURTNEY MILLER

Murder on the Royal Gorge Express

The Columbine Caper

Books may be purchased in quantity and/or special
sales by contacting the author or publisher at:
www.PopulvuhPublishing.com

Popul Vuh
Publishing

Book Design: Nick Zelinger, NZ Graphics
Book Consultant: Judith Briles, The Book Shepherd
Editing: Peggie Ireland

Published by Popul Vuh Publishing

ISBN: 978-1-949742-05-3 (Hardback)
ISBN: 978-1-949742-06-0 (Paperback)
ISBN: 978-1-949742-07-7 (e-Pub)
Library of Congress Control Number: 2020910088

1. Native American—Fiction 2. Cherokee—Fiction
3. White Feather (Fictitious Character)—Fiction 4. Murder
Investigation—Fiction 5. Wet Mountain Valley—Fiction

First Edition   Printed in USA

Acknowledgments

I want to thank the wonderful people who advised me on this book: my great friend Joanie Liebman who first suggested that I include the Columbine Club in a mystery; Addie Heck and Jennie Ness who met with Joanie and me to give me a feel for the spirit of the great ladies in the club; club members Judy Lynch, and Patty Pickerill; and especially Jacke Barnes who wrote the history of the club for its 100th anniversary in 2018.

The characters in the book are all fictional although I used the names of the founding ladies Maybell, Florence, Bessie, Lena, Theresa, and Elizabeth. I did not try to make my characters like those ladies but, instead, tried to put together a composite that represents the great spirit and spunk of the ladies I talked to in the club.

For details on the train and railroading in general, an important resource was my brother-in-law Lee Kessler who spent many years with the Santa Fe Railroad working in many positions including engineer and conductor. Joe Tosh of All Aboard Westcliffe and Larry Green with Pueblo Historical Society were two more helpful resources.

My daughter Mechelle and daughter-in-law Carey Miller rode the Royal Gorge Route with me at the beginning of my writing this story. And my mother Yetive Miller, my sister Connie and her husband Lee Kesler, my brother Mack Miller and his wife Kathy joined me to ride the Royal Gorge Route near the end of my writing so I could fill in some of the details of the train.

It is on that train ride when I met Acacia, a charming young lady on the Royal Gorge Route staff who was so nice and answered my silly questions about the specifics of the train. And thanks to Lynda at the Royal Gorge Route office who acquired permission for me to use the train as the main setting for the book. Note: for dramatic effect, I changed the name from Royal Gorge Route to Royal Gorge Express. But hopefully, most of the other details are accurate.

I want to thank Sheriff Shannon Byerly and his wife Lynette for their support and help with the book (and all books in the series).

I also want to thank the publishing team that helped put the book together: Dr. Judith Briles, The Book Shepherd; Nick Zelinger of NZ Graphics who designed the great cover and interior layouts; and the fantastic editor, Peggie Ireland.

*This book is dedicated to the incredible ladies of the
Custer County Columbine Club who celebrated
their club's 100th anniversary May 3, 2018.*

*Members attending: Judy Keyes, Jacke Barnes,
Joanie Liebman, Judy Papantonis, June Kilbourn,
Virginia Kness, Addie Heck, Paulie Canda, Barb Eberling,
Patty Pickerill, Anne Marie Donahoe, Pat Gibson,
Judy Lynch, Mary Horton, Linda Tyler, Sandy Dunlop,
Doris Porth, Kathy Boulee, Myrtle Schulze,
Gayle Bradburn, Nancy North, Gail Frickell,
Phyllis Dearborn, Monte Hess, and Carol Vimont.*

From the Award-Winning Author
COURTNEY MILLER
Murder on the Royal Gorge Express
The Columbine Caper
A White Feather Mystery

PART I:

[Monday] Presage

Chapter 1

Ready for the Raid

SHERIFF BAILEY SAT BACK in his chair. He was a tall man with broad shoulders, muscular build, and a happy, youthful appearance. "Okay, everyone understand the assignment?"

The deputies sitting around the table nodded grimly except for Deputy Jacobs who commented, "This is BIG."

Bailey acknowledged, "It is the biggest coordinated raid ever in the valley as far as I know."

Deputy Melton added, "Biggest one since I've been here."

Melton was the senior deputy having been part of the Wet Mountain Valley Sheriff's Office for going on thirty years. He had served under a number of sheriffs and had seen many changes in the valley during his three decades of service. He was short and thin, but his no-nonsense nature garnered the respect of his coworkers and the community.

After Colorado passed legislation to legalize marijuana in 2014, big commercial marijuana grow sites sprung up all across the state. Wet Mountain Valley opted out of allowing grow sites in its county so any grow sites in the valley were illegal. This created a huge challenge for the local sheriff's office because of the dense national forests of the foothills and mountains. Many sites were hidden in big houses originally built to be vacation homes but were now being rented by local criminals or by large cartels to hide wall-to-wall indoor crops. The cartels were well-funded and outmanned and outgunned the small local sheriff's office.

Deputy Sydney Jacobs lamented, "So, if legalizing marijuana was supposed to reduce illegal grow sites, why have they increased?"

Sheriff Bailey took it as rhetorical sarcasm, but Deputy Sam Morrison had a ready theory. "The sales tax and regulations make legal pot more expensive than the black market pot. Grow sites are easier to hide with so many legal ones scattered about. It's easier to move it around under the cover of legal stuff moving around as well."

Jacobs interpreted for herself. "So, it's easier to hide in plain sight."

Morrison was relatively new in the Wet Mountain Valley Sheriff's Office, but his years of experience as a homicide detective in Denver had elevated him into an informal leadership position. Jacobs was a young woman who was not pretty but attractive in a rugged, dangerous way. She had gained everyone's respect early on the job by her willingness to step forward and take charge when needed.

Melton added, "And the regulations have been slow in getting up to speed. A lot of loopholes still exist."

Sheriff Bailey did not want his staff to get too far into the politics so he reminded them, "Ours is not to reason why .... Meeting adjourned."

Undersheriff Buster Crab reminded them, "Go get some sleep. We have to be in position by 3:00 a.m."

The robust black man in his late sixties followed Bailey into his office. "You still gonna take off afterward?"

Bailey pushed back his cap. "If at all possible. I promised Pennie."

"Good. I think you should. We can handle the aftermath."

"I know you can, but it raises eyebrows."

"You mean Smiles?"

"Yeah, I guess so," Bailey answered reluctantly.

Colorado Bureau of Investigations agent S. Miles Blakeley was a thorn in the side of the Wet Mountain Valley Sheriff's Office. They called him Smiles behind his back not only because it combined his first initial and middle name but also because he never smiled. He had lost the respect of his colleagues because of his arrogance and gruff, abrasive manner that rubbed everyone the wrong way. They saw him as incompetent and power hungry. But, unfortunately, he was the CBI agent assigned to them and they often needed the help of the CBI and the resources it could provide.

"Shake it off. Nobody cares what he thinks. Besides, he is so stuck on himself, he'll never notice you're gone."

Sheriff Bailey chuckled, then asked seriously, "You ever ride the train, Buster?"

"Sure, fortieth anniversary. It was a lot of fun. Good food and a spectacular view of the Royal Gorge and the bridge."

"We just want to get away. Pennie took Randy's assignment pretty hard."

Buster clarified, "Randy is your youngest boy, right?"

"Yeah."

"Afghanistan, right?"

"Right."

"Jared served over there too, didn't he?"

"It's different. Jared is Navy."

"Is Randy Marines?"

"Yep. Just seems more dangerous."

Buster turned to leave. "She'll love the train. Do you both some good to get away."

Chapter 2

What Have I Done?

FRANK WAS WORRIED. SITTING next to Ralph Jacobs in Mrs. Barkley's office could not be good. He rifled through all recent events in his mind and was certain he had done nothing wrong or violated any rules. But after spending five years as a homeless vagabond in Canon City, he felt insecure sitting in the administrator's large office at St. Jude's. He had learned in the most tragic way that fortunes can turn unexpectedly. He did not want to go back to that former life.

St. Jude Methodist Retirement Center for the Indigent had rescued him and given him a good new life. It was too nice of a gig to give up. Not now that he had started to feel normal again. Not now that he had something to look forward to every day. Not now that he had good friends and a healthy social life.

Ralph Jacobs got to the point. "What's up?"

Mrs. Edith Barkley, the center's young, attractive administrator, sat up straight with a twinkle in her eye. "I have great news that I think you will really like. We have two rooms with a view that have opened up. Since both of you are in rooms with no outside windows, we thought you might like to move."

"We still have to share a bathroom?" Ralph asked.

"Well, all rooms here share a bathroom."

"No, I mean me and him." Ralph pointed an incriminating thumb at Frank.

Frank was taken aback at first, but then remembered that Ralph was the master of rudeness although he never meant to be. In his previous life, grumpy Ralph had owned a large construction firm. But, his divorce had left him without a business and too old to start over. Mrs. Barkley giggled and tried to regain her composure. "One of you would be sharing the bathroom with White Feather. The other room would not have a roommate at this point. It is the room across the hall from White Feather."

While Ralph thought about it, Frank remained silent. Ralph had been at St. Jude longer so Frank felt Ralph should have first choice. But Frank thought about the choices. He was not sure he wanted to share a bathroom with White Feather even though they were good friends. The old Cherokee elder was very strange so he was not sure he wanted to know him that intimately.

"What about Lizzie's room?" Ralph asked. "It's vacant."

Mrs. Barkley smiled and answered with a soft voice, "We don't allow men to share a bathroom with women."

"Why not? We ain't teenagers."

"No, but it is the rule and I agree with it. And I'm sure Ruth would not approve anyway."

"What about the room by the TV room? That's been empty since I've been here."

Mrs. Barkley had to think about it. "Oh. You mean the one that opens into the third floor TV and rec room?"

"Yeah. That room has a nice view and great access to the rec room."

"Well, we have just assumed that no one would want to have to pass through the rec room to get to their room. And what about the noise?"

"What noise? Nobody uses that room when the big screen is downstairs. It would be like having a big private living room."

Mrs. Barkley seemed lost in thought before answering cautiously. "If you are serious, Ralph, I will take it into consideration."

Ralph slapped the arms of his chair. "You through with me?"

Mrs. Barkley frowned, "Yes, but would you like to look at the rooms before you decide?"

Ralph pushed himself to his feet and turned to leave exclaiming, "Decided!"

Mrs. Barkley turned to Frank. "What about you, Frank?"

Now, Frank really had a dilemma. If he did not choose the room connected to White Feather's room, would White Feather be offended? And, if he chose the other room, would he get someone worse as a roommate later?

"Would you like to think about it, Frank?"

Feeling pressured, Frank asked, "The one across from White Feather have a view of the Sangres?"

Mrs. Barkley's eyes lit up. "Oh, yes, it is a magnificent view, Frank. Would you like to go down and look at the rooms?"

Frank studied the floor, then looked up and tilted his head to one side. "Let's do it."

The views from both rooms were magnificent. The room adjoining White Feather looked out over the verdant Wet Mountain Valley to the south. The other room looked out over the west plaza with the pond, the hill with the cemetery, and the Sangre de Cristo Mountains in the background.

"Definitely this one!" Frank proclaimed staring at the majestic mountain range.

This room was laid out differently than his current room. He liked this layout better. The door from the hallway opened up to the side of the room with the recliner and cabinets with the bed behind the door. The recliner was next to the window allowing him to stare out at the gorgeous mountains by just turning his head to the right. Across from the chair were cabinets mounted high above a small sink and mirror and a long counter with a small refrigerator below. A television sat at the opposite end of the counter above some drawers. The sink and mirror were in the main room because, unlike his current room, there was no vanity in the bathroom, only the toilet and shower.

Frank dropped down into the recliner and sighed. "Oh, this is perfect."

Mrs. Barkley confided, "I agree, Frank, this is very nice. When would you like to move in?"

"My calendar is open for this afternoon; or tomorrow anytime; or the next day ...."

Mrs. Barkley stopped him. "I will send TJ up to help you pack and move you in here this afternoon."

Chapter 3

Sam Alone

Deputy Sam Morrison pitched his keys into the wooden ashtray on the small end table by the bed and laid his cell phone beside it. He pulled off his badge and dropped it into the ashtray with the keys. The inner bowl of the relic was black from cigarettes being snuffed out over many years of use by his chain-smoking father. The stain was permanent; it could not be scrubbed off. The offensive smell lingered and gave Sam a chance to remember the stench of his father when held close for a sniff. It was almost all he had left from his father. The man had worked long hours day after day and died with few mementos to pass down to his large family.

He dug his wallet out of his hip pocket and laid it beside his cell phone. As he turned toward the closet, he loosened his belt buckle and let the weight of the gun belt slide off across his buttocks. He draped it over the arm of the easy chair in the corner like a saddle. His stomach was full after devouring a small pizza from Tony's washed down by a cold beer. It was a combination he hoped would make him sleepy. If he crashed now, he could get in six hours of sleep before having to rise for the raid. His assignment was one of two private residences in the southern part of the valley near the airport. The sheriff had said, "These are not Billy Bob's grow operations. These are highly scientific and technical grows." The houses had become suspicious when the local utility company noticed excessively high electrical bills in houses that were supposed to have only part-time residents.

The team was to meet in hanger number five at the airport at 3:00 a.m. to prepare for the coordinated assault. He would be matched with teams from CBI, DEA, and ICE. Surveillance had reported only two people ever visited the house. They always arrived in a maroon colored Silverado pickup truck. The assault method in the morning would depend upon whether the truck would be parked at the house or not.

Sam found himself nervous as he stripped down to his boxers. He was seldom part of a SWAT operation. He knew it could be explosive and dangerous, but that was not the source of his anxiety. He checked his watch. It was 7:45 p.m. His ex had promised to call him back at 7:30 p.m. She was seldom late for anything. He had called her around 3:00 p.m. that afternoon hoping to arrange a meeting with her at Tony's Pizza Place. She had been very short with him, but that was not unusual when he called her at work. He had told her he wanted to tell her something, but she had seemed disinterested in meeting at Tony's, instead telling him she would just call him later. They had settled on 7:30 that evening for her return call.

He dumped his clothes in the hamper, picked up his phone and dropped into the chair. Checking recent calls confirmed he had not missed hers. He dropped his hand on the arm rest, slid down and rested his head on the back of the chair.

The reason for his call earlier now seemed silly and trivial. After sitting through the dress rehearsals at the office all morning, he had a moment when the fear from the danger of the mission had sneaked up on him and left him wanting to reach out to Samantha just in case it was for the last time. Even while he was asking her to meet him for dinner, her curt response had reminded him how pathetic and melodramatic he was being. Now he was even dreading her call. After all, what was the "something" that he wanted to tell her? It seemed laughable.

The cell phone buzzed before he could rehearse a plausible reason for wanting to talk to her.

"Hi, Sam."

"Hi, Sam." Samantha inhaled as if out of breath. "What did you want to talk about?"

He sensed urgency and dread in her voice. She probably was thinking he wanted to talk about their relationship again and she was not in the mood. After the divorce Samantha and the kids had moved from Denver to Rockcliffe to get away from him. She had not been too happy when he had accepted the deputy position at the Wet Mountain Valley Sheriff's Office. Although seeing each other again had gotten off to a very shaky start, he had felt they were making some progress over the winter and spring going to their kids' school events together. Still, he had hoped for more.

"I just wanted to touch bases with you."

He heard a huff and there was a long pause before she insisted, "Well, I don't have much time, Sam. Is there something specific you wanted to say?"

It was Sam's turn to take a deep breath. "Sorry, Sam, I just wanted to let you know we are conducting valley-wide raids in the morning."

Samantha did not respond. Sam hurriedly added, "That's all. I just ...."

He heard Tammy in the background announce, "He's here, Mom."

The words penetrated his heart like daggers. "Was that Tammy?"

Samantha huffed again. "I have to go, Sam. These raids ... they affect me how?"

"Oh, they don't affect you. I'm sorry. We are raiding the illegal grow sites in the valley. It could be ... dangerous, you know?"

She was quiet but she did not have to say anything. It was obvious she was wondering why he was bothering her with it.

"I've really gotta go, Sam. Stay safe."

"Well, okay, I'll let you go. Sorry I bothered ..."

The sound of the phone going dead was like a metaphor for the deathlike feeling he had by being cut off by her. "He's here, Mom," he repeated out loud. "He?"

The shock of Samantha dating someone else left him stunned and hurting. Of course she could date someone else. They were divorced. He had no claim on her anymore. But, the surprising thing to him at that moment was that he had never considered she might ever date someone else.

She was young and very attractive. She had always been too pretty to be his girl. But, over time he had come to think she loved him, really loved him and no one else. They were a pair for ever and ever. They had vowed so when they married. And she had always been faithful and dedicated to him until he pushed her aside for his work. He had been faithful to her in that he had never looked at another woman. He had never had feelings for anyone else. But he had taken her for granted and dedicated himself to a new love—-the Denver P.D.

He had been certain that their divorce was about regaining his attention through the shock of separation. He never doubted that they were still in love, but he had neglected her and the kids and she was making a statement. He had expected her to throw her arms around him when he moved to Rockcliffe. He thought she would see that he was getting the message and responding.

Instead, she had been furious with him. Instead, she had avoided him and only grudgingly allowed him to reunite with the kids. Even the kids had not welcomed him back with open arms. They were protective of their mother and now he was an outsider. He had not given them the attention they deserved either.

Sam rubbed his face with his hands feeling the wetness of his eyes. He could not bear to think that it was really over. That it was final.

Sam Morrison would not sleep that night.

PART II:

[Tuesday] The Big Raid

Chapter 4

Awakened by the Raid

T HE ANCIENT FOUR-STORY building housing the St. Jude Methodist Retirement Center for the Indigent was deathly silent except for the raspy snoring of the residents in their rooms. In his dream, Frank Roberts was lying in a lush valley filled with tall grasses. In the distance he could hear whoosh, whoosh, whoosh, whoosh, whoosh ...

He could feel the pounding, sharp sounds in his chest. He dreamed of being surrounded by Canon City Parks crews hacking thick grasses and slowly working their way toward him. Fear gripped him as he imagined them hacking him to bits once they got to him sleeping on the park bench.

His eyes flew open. Faint light was passing through the window across the room. The whooshing sound was getting more and more pronounced. Lights were flashing in the distance coloring the window panes with greens and reds and blues. He rolled out of bed and trudged shakily to the window bumping into the recliner. As he felt his way around the large chair, he realized that the whooshing sounds were coming from a helicopter.

From the window he could see the flashing lights and barely make out the silhouette of the military-style chopper.

It was passing over St. Jude and heading west. More colorful flashing lights were coming from behind Cemetery Hill bulging to the west. Something big was going down.

Frank rubbed his eyes and looked again. It appeared that more flashing lights on the ground were moving fast to some point west of the retirement center to join with other stationary flashing lights.

The chill of the high altitude air made his skin feel icy. He moved back to his bed, found his robe, threw it on and then opened the door to enter the hallway. He saw White Feather standing with his arms crossed looking out the large hallway window to the west.

Frank joined him. "What is it?" he asked.

His elderly Native American friend answered simply, "Raid."

"Raid? A police raid?"

White Feather did not answer. Then Frank remembered. "The grow site?"

White Feather glanced at Frank and then closed his eyes. Frank sensed it was the Indian's polite way of saying yes without having to speak. Frank remembered how he came to know about the grow site. It had all started when his gang of old geezer friends had found a metal box buried in the basement of St. Jude. When they were unable to pry it open, Ralph had assured them that he could open it.

The geezers had assumed that Ralph was leaning on his background in construction. It turned out that he was drawing on his experience in the military. He had instructed them to carry the box up over Cemetery Hill to the back of the St. Jude property where he had rolled a soft, doughlike substance he called C4 into a long thin rope and wrapped it around the lid. Frank had recognized C4 as the name of a plastic explosive he had seen in the military.

Ralph had expertly placed two wire probes into the soft compound, unrolled the wire and connected them to a small detonator box. Hurriedly, White Feather had elbowed the others behind an old stone well for protection. They ducked down as Ralph detonated the explosive. When they looked up the box was gone. White Feather had been first to spot it hurtling toward the ground.

They had chased after the box and found it in a crater inside a marijuana grow site surrounded by Concertina wire. Rough-looking Latino men in camouflage uniforms carrying assault rifles came running up and spotted the old men. Amid a hail of gunfire, the old men had scrambled back to the safety of St. Jude and vowed never to speak of it again.

"It's the grow site, isn't it?"

White Feather opened his eyes and glared at Frank and then nodded toward the door to his room. Once inside, White Feather stated in a hushed voice, "Could be good; could be bad."

"Okay. What's the good news?"

"Put 'em in jail."

"The bad news?"

"Think we turned 'em in."

"Oh!" Frank did not like that. "But it has been months."

White Feather did not respond. He seldom did.

"Should we tell the others?"

"No."

Frank nodded and returned to his room filled with fear and dread. He was no longer sleepy so he stood by his window to watch the flashing lights and circling helicopter. An intense beam of light streamed out of the nose of the chopper and danced around as if writing a message on the ground. In time, the chopper disappeared behind Cemetery Hill. Because the flashing lights persisted without movement, the chopper must have set down. After a while with no sign of action, Frank got tired and checked the clock. It was 4:35 a.m.

He switched on the TV and dropped into his recliner. His mind could not focus on the TV. He wondered why White Feather was being so secretive other than the fear that the thugs in camouflage might come after them. He wondered if there was something more sinister but could not imagine what it would be.

With White Feather it could be anything. Albert Stein, who had once been a newspaper reporter, had told him that White Feather was a Cherokee medicine man with a mysterious past. Albert was clearly intrigued and Frank was sure that Albert would someday get the old Indian to open up. The lyrics from an old Beatles song flashed into his mind. "He must be so good looking because he is so hard to see."

The song's words summed up White Feather. He must be really magical and wise because he is so solemn and enigmatic. Frank smiled. *Unlike myself. I am more like the Mark Twain quip, "better to keep your mouth shut and appear stupid than open your mouth and remove all doubt." I am constantly removing all doubt* Frank thought to himself and chuckled.

Squirming to improve his comfort in the soft recliner, Frank slipped into a nice early morning nap.

Chapter 5

Shadows in the Kitchen

RALPH JACOBS HAD DONE this many times. He woke up hungry at 4:00 a.m. and ignored the St. Jude curfew to wander down to the first floor kitchen. Having been a construction engineer in his previous life, he noticed the complete silence on his journey from his room on the third floor. He knew that this was possibly the only time during the day that the temperature stabilized and the old building was settled and completely quiet. It was that rare time when the building was not responding to temperature changes by creaking from expansion or contraction.

The grumpy, stooped old man crossed the dining room to look out the large windows at the moonlit night. Standing on the first floor, he gazed at the black mound that was known to the residents as Cemetery Hill. It was really just a silvery, rounded obstacle blocking the valley. He noticed the auroralike hues glowing just above the rounded hill and assumed they were the northern lights. For a moment he remembered his father waking him up and dragging him outside to see the Aurora Borealis. It had not impressed him other than to think "Is that all it is?" That was a long time ago. Tonight he was hungry and his grumbling stomach sounded deafening in the total silence. He resumed his quest to find a late night snack.

He stopped short at the sound of rustling to his right. A glint of light caught his eye. Must be a reflection. Maybe something metal like a belt buckle? Was that a person backed up to the wall standing perfectly still? The shock of it transported him back many years to Korea and one late night when he was heading to the chow hall sensing the enemy hiding in the shadows of the night.

As he had that night, he once again felt totally vulnerable in the open waiting for the kill shot that curiously never came. Just as he had done that night long ago, Ralph numbly moved forward ignoring the threat looming only feet away. His nerves were on edge. He sensed someone crouching behind the drink cart.

Ralph inched forward keeping his head straight and using only peripheral vision. Why hadn't they shot him? Why were they hiding? Were they preparing to ambush the camp? Were they just spying on his platoon? He kept moving forward and pushed through the swinging door into the kitchen where he hoped to be safe. He heard rustling noises and sensed someone in the room scurrying for cover to his left. He forced himself to ignore whoever it was and instead headed straight for the large industrial refrigerator to his right.

A metal utensil fell making a loud clanking noise in the back of the room. Someone gasped almost imperceptibly. Why were they afraid of him? He was old and unarmed after all. He opened the refrigerator door allowing a stream of light to illuminate the room. Shadows ducked back out of the light. He took a deep breath and stayed the mission fearing any sign that he was aware of them would bring the enemy down on him. As long as he did not acknowledge that he knew of their presence maybe he would be safe. It had worked that night in Korea.

He opened a container filled with tuna fish sandwiches and purloined a couple setting them on a shelf to enable him to close and replace the container. Cradling the sandwiches against his stomach, he closed the refrigerator door and slipped back through the swinging door of the kitchen through the dining room and back into the corridor. He paused to catch his breath. He had made it. He was safe again.

That night years ago, he had managed to rouse his platoon for an attack. They had only found three unarmed gooks hiding near the chow hall and they had been shot without question. He had since wondered if they were just hungry villagers searching for a meal. So many tragedies, so many killed senselessly in that conflict.

His heart was racing; his mind in high gear. Had tonight really happened? Had there really been people in the kitchen or had he just imagined it? If it was real, who could they have been?

No, something had prompted old war memories. They had a fancy name for flashbacks nowadays. Even at his advanced age, he was not completely over the horrors he had experienced in the war. It still haunted him and forever would. He would never forget the "Forgotten War." Ralph shook it off and returned to his new room for his snack. But, the pangs of hunger had been joined by the lingering pangs of fear. He retrieved a beer from the little refrigerator and strolled out to one of the comfortable Victorian-style chairs placed in front of the small television. He clicked on the TV and attacked the sandwiches ravenously and downed the beer with loud gulps.

With bread crumbs and mayonnaise-laden tuna fish littering his chest and belly, Ralph burped and almost immediately began snoring loudly.

Chapter 6

Sydney Visits Grampa

THE RAID HAD BEEN chaotic and terrifying. Amidst gunfire, exploding canisters, shouting, bright spotlights, three members of the cartel residing on-site were seen escaping out a back gate and ten others quickly surrendered. The compound was systematically secured and prisoners were now being transported to the Fremont County facilities.

Deputy Sydney Jacobs had felt a rush like she had never felt before. Previously, she had wondered if she would have the courage to step up in a gunfight. Now she knew that she could not only overcome her fear but actually thrived under the intensity of combat. Now she knew that, in fact, she liked being a part of a team in a life-threatening battle. She was proud of her performance. She would never have doubts about confronting danger again.

With the site secure, unessential personnel were released. As Sydney pulled away from the scene her heart was still racing and her energy level so high that the thought of returning to the mundane routine awaiting her was insufferable. She needed to share the incredible early morning experience with someone. She needed to brag about her triumph in combat.

She checked her watch and determined that her grandfather, Ralph Jacobs, would be heading for breakfast soon.

She would be passing by St. Jude on her way back to the office but she had mixed emotions about visiting her grandfather. She felt obligated since she was the only family he had left that would look in on him. Ralph Jacobs was often angry and insulting, sometimes grumpy and rude, but occasionally, actually quite rarely, he could be tender and thoughtful. Although she dreaded each visit beforehand, she always felt good afterward. And now she thought he'd be just the person in her life who would appreciate her feelings. After all, he was ex-military. Maybe her job could connect them on a new level.

Ralph had had a very hard life. His ex-wife had been a demanding and offensive alcoholic. She managed to take his construction business in the divorce settlement, which left Ralph, already up in years, to work odd construction jobs until his health finally failed him.

Sydney's father had not had a good relationship with Ralph and no longer tried to have a relationship at all. So, when Ralph could no longer work, Sydney had felt obligated to take responsibility for him and had pulled some strings to get him admitted into St. Jude. It was nice, in a way, for Sydney since she lived only a few miles south of St. Jude in Rockcliffe. Her close proximity also took away any excuse for not dropping by for a visit periodically.

Naomi, the receptionist, let her through to go up to his room. Sydney was surprised to learn he had moved. She found her grumpy grampa sitting in a small TV room on the third floor in a soft, high-backed chair fast asleep with the television blaring. She walked over and pushed his unruly hair out of his face. He seemed so peaceful, she hesitated to wake him.

She walked over and switched off the noisy television. Ralph awoke immediately. "Whoozare?"

"It's just me Grampa. Came by to see how you're doing."

Ralph rubbed his face with his palms and struggled to get his bearings.

"I hear you got a new room." Ralph threw out his arms. There was a gleam in his eyes and he almost smiled. "What d'ya think?"

Sydney glanced around at the public TV room. "This?"

"Comes with the room." He pointed his thumb over his shoulder.

Sydney walked over to the open door on the south side of the TV room and looked in. It was disheveled like her grandfather, but behind the mess she could see that it was a very nice room with a window and great view of the Sangre de Cristo Mountains.

She walked into the room. "Fabulous view, Grampa!"

Ralph shuffled into the room behind her. "Really? What do you see?"

"The mountains!"

"Oh, yeah, that." He dropped down into the soft worn recliner. "Take a look around if you want. It's nicer than the old place."

"Yes, I see that." She glanced into the shared bathroom not surprised to find it a mess as well. She picked up the discarded towel from the floor and hung it on the towel rack beside the shower and closed the shower door.

"What d'ya think?" he asked again revealing a touch of pride.

Sydney confirmed saying, "So much nicer than the other place. Do you like it?"

His face broke into a brief smile and then a frown. "Not bad. Not bad. The guys are jealous."

"I would think so. How did you ..."

Ralph snickered. "How did an old grump like me get such a nice place?"

He beamed and said, "I asked for it. I think Mrs. Barkley wanted to stick me in with that Injun, but I insisted on this place."

"Well, I really like it, Grampa. Maybe I should come live with you."

Ralph snorted. "Gonna hafta put on a few more miles before you can break into this place."

Sydney giggled at his remark and sat down on the edge of the bed.

Ralph jumped up and waved his arms as if herding flies. "You don't hafta sit on the bed granddaughter. We have a nice parlor now." They adjourned to the couch in the TV Room.

He always asked, "Shoot anybody lately?"

Before that day she had responded no and dreaded the day she would have to say yes. But today, she slapped her holstered pistol with her hand. "Nope, but I'm ready. Just gimme an excuse."

Ralph laughed. She loved it when he laughed, but it seemed so unnatural for him.

"Did you hear about the big raid?"

"Raid?"

"It was BIG, Grampa! Nationwide. We raided three places in the valley and Fremont County hit a half dozen more."

"Big speed trap?"

It was Sydney's turn to laugh. "No. Illegal marijuana grow sites."

"I thought it was legal in Colorady."

"It is in some places. Each county has to approve it. It ain't legal in Wet Mountain Valley."

"Three sites, eh? That's a lot for your little office."

"Oh, it wasn't just us. We had the CBI, DEA, BLM, ICE ..."

Ralph snarled, "IBD."

"IBD? What's that, Grampa?"

"I'll Be Darned."

Sydney laughed. "We even had some armored vehicles and a Black Hawk helicopter. You would have loved it. We had explosives to blow the doors off and smoke canisters."

There was a little twinkle Sydney perceived in Ralph's eye when she mentioned explosives.

"Bring me any C4? I'm running out."

"We don't use that, Grampa. Besides, you better not have any. I would have to haul you in and put you in with the Cubans we captured."

But then Ralph became thoughtful, perhaps even worried. "Any of 'em get away?"

"Yeah, actually, three Cuban nationals got away just over the hill." She pointed west toward the site.

Ralph's eyes grew large. "It was real!" He looked at Sydney with wild eyes. "When was it?"

"Around 4:00 a.m."

He gripped the chair arms. "They were here!"

"You saw them?"

"I thought it was that PFCHD stuff happening to me again."

"PFCHD?

Ralph waved his hand. "Whatever it's called. You know, shell shock."

"Oh, PTSD, post-traumatic stress disorder."

"Whatever. I was down in the kitchen last night to get a sandwich."

Sydney giggled. "So I see. You're still wearing most of it." She pointed at the crumbs on his shirt.

He half-heartedly brushed off his shirt. "I thought I heard something in the darkness. It looked like a belt buckle sparkling. Then I thought I heard shuffling in the kitchen. I thought I was imagining it. You know, flashbacks from Korea."

Sydney touched his arm. "I think it might have been our fugitives, Grampa."

"I should've shot 'em."

"What with?" Then Sydney reached for her radio.

Ralph shook his head and cussed under his breath, while Sydney radioed a report to dispatch.

Sydney Checks Out Burglary

"I NEED TO SEARCH THE place."

Ralph proudly followed his granddaughter around St. Jude like a faithful puppy. They started in the dining room and kitchen. The scrumptious aroma of frying bacon and eggs attacked Sydney's nostrils and made her stomach yearn for food, suddenly realizing that she was famished.

Ralph led her through the dining room and said, "One was over there." Ralph pointed at a drink cart. "The other one was hiding in that nook . . . the one with the shiny belt buckle."

Sydney studied the two areas he pointed out searching for any sign to corroborate her grampa's report. Finding nothing she asked, "The other one was in the kitchen?"

Ralph led her through the double swinging doors into the kitchen. Smoke from the grill billowed out bombarding them with smells so vibrant that she could almost taste the greasy, succulent treat sizzling on the commercial-sized grill. Ralph pointed to the left, but Sydney's eyes were stuck on Birdie standing over the grill with a spatula poking and flipping the bacon. "I heard him over there. He knocked over some metal pot or something."

Birdie swung around so forcefully that her spatula flew out of her hand and across the room. Sydney ducked behind a table and cringed at the sound of the metal utensil ricocheting off the swinging door and onto the floor.

"Lawsy me!" Birdie shouted. She slapped her cheeks and opened her mouth wide and broke into an infectious belly laugh. Sydney stood tentatively and waved sheepishly. Birdie declared, "You almost scared me out of my skin, girl."

Sydney held up her hands, "I'm sorry, Birdie. Grampa was just showing me where he saw some strangers last night."

Birdie's eyes got big. "I's about to calls you, Deputy. Someone stole half our stock last night. The icebox is nearly empty."

Sydney made a note as she explained, "I think it was the fugitives from the raid last night. I think Grampa may have heard them. He's showing me where he thinks they were hiding."

Birdie gave Ralph the evil eye. "You seen 'em and you didn't say nothing?"

Ralph cowered behind the metal table. "I wasn't sure I'd seen 'em! I did hear noises in the kitchen. I just wasn't sure."

Sydney defended him. "He thought he was having a flashback. You know, PTSD from the war."

Now Birdie looked at him sympathetically and then cackled like an old hen. "So why was you in my kitchen in the middle of the night?"

Ralph looked sheepishly at her and simply replied, "I was hungry."

Birdie addressed Sydney, "So, who was those thugs?"

"Last night a joint task force of FBI, CBI, Fremont County Sheriff's Office, and a SWAT team raided about a dozen illegal marijuana grow sites. One of them was located behind St. Jude." She pointed west. "Three Cubans escaped out the back and got away. It must have been them that stole food out of your refrigerator."

Ralph interrupted with, "Here's a ladle on the floor. That's what he must have knocked down. That's what I heard!"

Sydney and Birdie rushed over to see for themselves. Ralph puffed up as if feeling vindicated. Sydney put down a marker. "We'll check it for fingerprints."

"So you were over by the refrigerator, Grampa?"

"I took two sandwiches out of a container and then left."

Birdie waggled her finger at him. "I knowed it was you poaching them sandwiches at night."

Birdie went back to the grill and scooped the bacon off and placed them on a plate and then waddled over to the refrigerator and threw open the door. "Looky here, Sydney, this was full last evening!"

The refrigerator was barely half full now. "They stole that much?"

"Shore did!"

Sydney made a note and then reached up and keyed her mic. "Gabby, Sydney here. We've got a 10-15 out here ..."

"A what?"

"10-15."

"What's that?"

"Look it up and report it to the CBI."

"Where are you?"

Sydney huffed. "Look it up, Gabby. I checked in, remember? Jacobs out."

Jacobs was frustrated. She felt like her coworkers were too easy going and lacked professionalism and sophistication. This was no time to be careless over the radio. "I need to speak to the administrator," Sydney stated, getting back to business.

Her Grampa snapped to attention and saluted, "Yes, sir. Follow me, sir."

Sydney and Birdie cracked up. "Sorry, Grampa."

Ralph shrugged it off. Birdie looked up at the wall clock. "She probably ain't in yet. Naomi should be though. She can get her on the horn for you."

"Yes, I saw Naomi when I came in. Can you get me an inventory of what's missing, Birdie?"

"Oh, yessum, no problem."

On the way to reception, Sydney was thinking out loud. "We will need to do a search of the premises. We will want to dust for prints. We should check the back door to see how they got in. I should get ahold of the sheriff ..."

When Sydney stormed through the door to reception she found Naomi Johnson sitting at her desk doing paperwork. "Oh, Sydney, you startled me!"

"Sorry, Naomi, but there's been a break in and I need to speak to Mrs. Barkley ASAP."

"Oh, Heavens. Anybody hurt?"

"I don't think so, but we should do a bed check immediately."

Naomi was obviously flustered by the news and seemed to be at a loss for what to do first.

Ralph checked his watch. "See ya."

Sydney was rattled by his sudden adieu. "Where are you going?"

"Time for breakfast!"

Sydney's stomach reacted to his declaration and she added, "I'll join you in a minute."

Chapter 8

Breakfast

Frank joined his friends for breakfast in the large dining room on the first floor. They were at their usual table in front of one of the ceiling to floor windows looking out over the west plaza. "This is my new view!"

He could see that his friends were confused, so he explained, "Mrs. Barkley has let me move into another room. It is on the west side and I now have this very view out my window."

Walter Montgomery applauded happily, and Albert Stein smiled and declared, "That is wonderful, Franklin."

Frank added, "I think it is the same view you and White Feather have, Albert."

White Feather nodded. Albert asked, "Which room is it, Franklin?"

"The one across the hall from White Feather."

"Oh, yes." Albert Stein was a small, fragile man who carried himself with distinction and character. He had been an investigative reporter for *The Denver Post* newspaper, but had fallen onto hard times when his wife had contracted cancer. After her passing, he was left bankrupt and getting accepted into St. Jude had saved him from being homeless.

Walter Montgomery, a large, rotund, happy man, was a former veterinarian. Although he had been excellent at his profession, he had not been a good businessman and had lost his practice. He had spent the rest of his productive years working for a large buffalo ranch. After a failed marriage, he found himself destitute.

Ralph sauntered up and slid his tray of food onto the table and tossed his napkin and silverware beside it. As he was pulling back his chair, Frank asked, "How you like your new room, Ralph?"

"Fine."

"Which room, Rudolph?" Albert asked.

"Rec room."

Frank explained, "Ralph asked for that room because it opens into the TV room on our floor. I thought he was crazy, at first, but after thinking about it, it makes a lot of sense. As you said, Ralph, it is like having a huge private living room."

Ralph had already stuffed his mouth with scrambled eggs, but proclaimed, "Party at seven."

Albert's face brightened as he asked his eating companions, "Did any of you gentlemen see the flashing lights last night?"

Ralph egged him on saying, "You see another UFO?"

Albert was indignant. "No, Rudolph, there must have been an emergency over in the valley behind Cemetery Hill. I counted a dozen emergency vehicles."

"You see the helicopter?" Frank blurted out before thinking. He glanced tentatively at White Feather. White Feather seemed unmoved.

"Th-There was a he-helicopter? F-Flight f-for Life maybe?" Walter questioned.

"Sikorsky Black Hawk." Ralph corrected.

Everyone, even White Feather, paused to study the wrinkled old veteran. Frank asked, "Military?"

Ralph responded nonchalantly, "FBI."

Albert put the pieces together. "The grow site! They raided that illegal grow site."

He turned to White Feather. "Did you see it, White Feather?"

White Feather nodded. "Joint raid."

As if on cue, Birdie approached. "You Sleuthkateers hear about the raids last night?"

Albert responded, "What do you know about it, Mrs. Beaudreau?"

"FBI, CBI, local Sheriff's office, Fremont County Sheriff's Office. Lordy, it was all over. They busted a dozen places in the Wet Mountain Valley and Fremont County."

"Where did you hear that?"

"Deputy Jacobs is here this morning. Three of the bums raided our ice box last night."

Ralph kept eating but declared, "I seen 'em!"

"What did you say, Rudolph?"

"I seen 'em! I told Sydney about it."

"Who was here?"

"The escaped Cubans."

Albert tried to get clarification. "So you actually saw them, Rudolph?

"Yep. I told Sydney. She reported it."

Frank asked, "Where were they when you saw them?"

Ralph paused to glance at Birdie. He shifted in his chair. "Well, I got hungry last night so I came down here to the kitchen to sneak a couple of sandwiches."

Birdie waggled her finger at him. "A couple?"

Ralph ignored her and continued, "I sensed several people lurking in the shadows over by the carts," he pointed toward the carts, "and another one in the kitchen!"

"Wearin' camouflage?" White Feather inquired.

"Couldn't tell in the dark."

Birdie waved her hands in the air, "Lordy! I hope they's not hiding in St. Jude's somewheres."

The Sleuthkateers, except for White Feather, jerked their heads around searching the room. White Feather calmly remarked, "They would be gone by now."

Ralph added, "Sydney is checking."

Birdie shook her head and headed back to the kitchen. "They'd better be. I gots my pistol in my purse and I ain't afraid to use it. We calls 9-1-1 afterwards around here."

Birdie stopped to wave her hand at the buffet line. "Helps yourself, Sydney."

Sydney helped herself to a plate full of bacon, eggs and toast, grabbed an orange juice off the drink tray and joined her grampa at his table. "Mind if I join you, gentlemen?"

The old geezers jumped to their feet. "Please do, Deputy."

Sydney sat down and glanced around the table. "As you were, gentlemen." They sat back down.

Albert asked first, "What can you share with us about the raids, Deputy Jacobs?"

Sydney scooped up a forkful of scrambled eggs, stuffed it into her mouth followed by a bite of bacon and answered,

"Well, I shouldn't say anything until the official announcement, so you gotta promise to keep it to yourselves."

As she washed it down with orange juice, the Sleuthkateers all promised to keep quiet. Sydney filled her mouth again, and gave them the scoop. "Last night a joint task force of DEA, FBI, CBI, local Sheriff's offices, and SWAT teams raided about a dozen illegal marijuana grow sites in the valley. Three from the Cuban cartel got away."

Albert clarified, "So, the grow site west of St. Jude is owned by a Cuban cartel?"

Sydney nodded and then gulped down the rest of her orange juice. Frank jumped up. "Let me get you a refill."

Ralph handed him his glass. Frank snapped it out of his hand and picked up Sydney's glass. "Wait 'till I get back to continue."

Albert filled the void. "We saw the lights flashing very early this morning. What time did you start the raids?"

"Three a.m. Caught them by surprise."

Frank rushed up and set the juice glasses down. "What'd I miss?"

Albert smiled like a patient father. "The raid started at 3:00 a.m."

Sydney gulped down more orange juice. "We went in with full shock and awe, blew open the gate, launched smoke grenades, the Black Hawk lit it up like daytime. There was gunfire and our targets were running around like headless chickens."

She reloaded her fork with eggs. "It was over in seconds."

The old geezers were speechless except for White Feather. "You see 'em escape?"

"Yeah, I reported it!" Sydney answered. "Saw 'em sneaking out the back gate. SWAT went after 'em."

Sydney had now eaten every morsel. Ralph dumped his leftovers onto her plate and Sydney devoured that helping. She drank the rest of her orange juice and then slapped her hands down on the table. "I want to see the back door ... figure out how they got in."

Chapter 9

Scary Man on the Hill

AFTER BREAKFAST, FRANK NEEDED to take a walk. His friends were preoccupied with Deputy Jacobs' investigation. He found it boring. He wondered if there might still be flashing lights at the grow site but remembered that Cemetery Hill would block any view. So he headed out the back door to the park bench in the west plaza. Today it would be a peaceful spot to look out over the small pond with the beautiful Sangre de Cristo Mountain Range in the distance.

Before he sat, he glanced up at the window of his new room on the third floor. He then turned to stare at the Sangre de Cristo Mountains rising up above the rounded hill to the west. His heart leaped at the memory of his new view. He had never realized just how claustrophobic his old room had been. Maybe because it had been such a giant step up from the refrigerator crate he had lived in before St. Jude.

It was cool sitting in the shadows of the great St. Jude building. He was enjoying the quiet and the view alone but hoped White Feather might join him so they could talk more about the raid.

Frank's mind drifted as his eyes searched for any flashing lights beyond Cemetery Hill. In the morning sun, there was no hint of any activity to the west. His eyes dropped to the twisted juniper trees next to the pond in front of the bench. He was a practical man and did not believe in time travel. But White Feather was determined to convince him that his special form of synesthesia meant that he could not only "see" time but also travel back in time when the portal opened up periodically.

Frank focused on the strange tree. Although it did look like one tree repeated three times, he did not believe that the time portal had caused the aberration. He believed it was three trees that looked alike but were just different sizes.

Frank crossed his legs and the bench shifted. The roots of the trees reached out just below the surface of the ground like thick veins causing the ground to be uneven beneath the bench. The shifting never seemed to bother White Feather, but it irritated Frank. He stood and examined the ground. Perhaps if he repositioned the bench he could find a spot where the bench would be stable. After numerous tries, at last he figured out how to situate the legs of the bench between the roots.

He sat and smiled proudly when the bench did not shift as he crossed his legs again. He cast his gaze back to the majestic mountains. The Sangre de Cristos were jagged and rugged mountains normally striking sharp silhouettes against a deep blue sky, but this morning puffy white clouds lay like soft thick blankets across the central peaks. He had read that this portion of the range boasted ten peaks over fourteen thousand feet high.

In the corner of his peripheral vision, something moved. He turned his attention toward Cemetery Hill, behind the pond covered by thick shrubs and trees. A man stood atop the hill in the shadows of a Douglas fir. His imposing stature startled Frank!

The man was large and tall with dark brown skin. He wore khaki pants and shirt and a wide-brimmed canvas hat. A combat-style rifle was draped casually over his shoulder and he leaned with his outstretched arm against the fir tree. He appeared to be locked in an ominous stare upon Frank. When Frank stared back, the man moved back into the shadows.

Frank felt that he had seen the man before, but where? Then it hit him! When he and his buddies had stumbled upon the illegal grow site just outside the western boundary of St. Jude, the man now standing atop the hill was one of the men that had run out, spotted them and started shouting and shooting at them.

He tried to pretend he had not seen the man and forced his eyes away only furtively glancing back to check on him. Two more heads were moving around in the depths of the shadows. Frank sensed they were gathering their things in preparation for something. They wasted no time scurrying away.

Frank felt a hand on his shoulder and jumped up screaming. White Feather folded over laughing. Frank panted trying to calm himself. "They … are … up … there!" He pointed toward the small clearing.

White Feather became immediately concerned and stared in the direction Frank pointed. Frank explained, "There are three of them, one in Khakis and the other two in camouflage. The one in Khakis has an assault weapon. They gathered up their stuff and took off."

White Feather pulled out his cell phone and called the sheriff's office to report it as he stomped off toward the clearing.

"We shouldn't ..." Frank began, but White Feather was leaving him behind. He rushed after him as if tethered to him with an invisible rope. White Feather's lack of hesitation gave Frank a sense of security that he knew in his mind was unwarranted. But, there was not time for sober thought, this was an emergency.

As they approached the steepest portion of the climb, Short of breath, Frank tried reason. "Should we go get Deputy Jacobs?"

"She's gone."

Chapter 10

Reconnoiter

FRANK WAS OUT OF breath, but White Feather's breathing was normal. Frank was certain that White Feather had to be late eighties, or even older. Not because he looked that age. He looked much younger, maybe seventies, but because Albert was certain that the Indian was quite ancient. "He knows the early twentieth century too well," Albert had shared. "In fact, he knows the nineteenth century too well for that matter."

Frank pointed to the spot where he had seen the man with the rifle. Thick shrubs surrounded the small clearing providing a natural hideaway. In the center were areas where the grass was flattened or pine needles swept away. White Feather knelt and examined the three spots. "Slept here," he suggested. He stood and walked a few steps. "Went north."

The old Indian looked toward the west. In the distance would be the illegal grow site. White Feather headed that way. Frank attempted to follow the spry old man.

After venturing across the top of Cemetery Hill westward, they came to the stone wall, old well, and crumbling foundation where they had attempted to blow the lid off the metal box. Frank stopped to sit on the crumbling foundation for a moment. White Feather stopped at the broken gate in the wall and stared in the direction of the grow site. Frank managed to ask, "See anything?"

"SUVs, SWAT vehicles, authorities."

Frank joined White Feather and they ventured off the St. Jude property to get a closer look. They were able to slip up to the fence that surrounded the grow site without detection and stand behind a shed. They could hear a familiar voice.

"Sheriff?" Frank whispered.

White Feather nodded and placed his finger to his lips.

"You need us anymore, Miles?"

"Didn't need you before."

"Smiles." Frank mouthed. White Feather confirmed with a nod.

Agent S. Miles Blakeley was the local Colorado Bureau of Investigations Agent stationed in Pueblo. Frank knew him as the arrogant man that had helped with the investigation of a poisoning at St. Jude. No one, and especially not any local Sheriff's officers, liked the rude, egotistical agent.

"Okay, guys, wrap it up," Sheriff Bailey commanded his deputies. White Feather led Frank around the compound to a deputy's SUV. Deputy Bill Melton was surprised to see them walk up.

"White Feather!"

"Deputy."

Senior Deputy Bill Melton had taken a liking to White Feather while working with him on the Ludwig case and had used his connections in the Methodist Church to get White Feather admitted to St. Jude. Melton looked east in the direction of the retirement center. "What brings you two over here?"

"Saw the lights last night."

Melton locked eyes on them. "You know about this place?"

White Feather did not answer. Frank followed his lead. Melton nodded. "Cartel."

"Cartel?" Frank questioned.

"Cuban cartel, we think."

"Get 'em?" White Feather asked.

"Got most of them, but the boss and a couple others managed to slip out the back."

Frank's stomach tightened. He looked to White Feather, but the stoic man gave no reaction. Melton continued, "You ain't seen anybody suspicious over your way have you?"

"They head our way?"

Melton shook his head. "Don't know, maybe."

He looked directly at White Feather and said, "Keep vigilant. They are dangerous men."

"Got anybody looking for 'em?"

"Oh, yeah, SWAT team from Pueblo. They think they must have headed north. More cover up there in the forests and rocks."

White Feather pointed east. "Camped up there."

Melton looked surprised. "You see 'em?"

"Maybe."

Melton reached through the SUV window for the mic.

Frank was not satisfied. "Sheriff sending anyone over to guard St. Jude?"

"I doubt it. No reason to believe they would risk being seen over there.

Sheriff Bailey strolled up. "What are you doin' over here, White Feather?"

"Hunting."

Bailey and Melton broke into laughter. "Had any luck?"

"No game, just animals."

"Same as us! You see Deputy Jacobs at your place?"

White Feather folded his arms and nodded.

Melton seemed surprised. "Sydney over at St. Jude?"

Bailey nodded and tapped his radio. "Her grandfather may have seen or at least heard them when he was raiding the refrigerator for a snack. She found where someone had jimmied the back door."

Melton pointed his head toward White Feather. "White Feather thinks our fugitives may have camped on the hill west of St. Jude."

Bailey asked, "You see 'em?"

White Feather pointed his thumb at Frank. Frank responded, "I saw three men up on Cemetery Hill. One watched me while the others gathered up their stuff and then they took off."

White Feather clarified, "Headed north."

Bailey looked at Melton. "That's why SWAT missed 'em. They headed east initially while SWAT headed north. Now the Cubans are behind the SWAT team heading north."

Sheriff Bailey studied White Feather. "Notify Smiles about the campsite." Melton reached for the mic again and radioed in the report.

Bailey asked Frank, "What'd they look like?"

"One wore khaki shirt and pants, carried an assault rifle. The other two wore camouflage."

"That's them all right." He turned to Melton. "You know I'm going to be out of pocket tomorrow. I need you to help Buster keep the peace in the valley."

"You still going on the train ride?"

"Yeah, I promised Pennie and Smiles thinks we're in the way."

Melton shook his head. "Jerk."

"Train ride?" White Feather asked.

"Yeah, we're going to take a ride on the Royal Gorge Express over in Canon City. Ever done that?"

White Feather shook his head.

"Supposed to be pretty cool. They serve dinner and every-thing. You should try it sometime."

White Feather looked north toward Canon City. "I will."

Melton replaced the mic and cautioned the sheriff, "Keep an eye out for our fugitives. They're probably headed that way."

"Pennie will shoot me if I even think about work tomorrow."

He looked at Frank and gave him a reassuring smile. "I'll have someone keep an eye on St. Jude."

Sheriff Bailey called the deputies to the conference table. "Okay, remember our first responsibility is to keep the peace in the valley. So, except for the search team assigned to CBI, we are back to our normal routines. Just keep an eye out for reports of strangers and pass it on to the CBI."

Sydney reminded him. "I reported that Grampa seen 'em, at least heard 'em, at St. Jude after the raid."

"Yes, I saw that report and dispatch sent it over to Smiles' group. White Feather and Roberts also spotted them on Cemetery Hill this morning. We believe they headed north from there."

"Shouldn't we post someone at St. Jude? I could hang around over there today."

"I need you to run up to San Isabel and check out that abandoned car with Ranger Jack like we talked about, Sydney. Buster and I'll see what we can do to cover St. Jude. Remember, I'm not going to be around tomorrow, so I need everyone to be on their toes."

Undersheriff Crab joined in, "We got this, Sean. You just go have a good time and forget about this place for one day.

Chapter 11

New Resident

Trying to keep up with White Feather had left Frank exhausted. After a shower and short nap, he caught up with his friends carrying their food trays to their usual spot at lunch. He was eager to update them on his and White Feather's discoveries. But, just as they were all getting settled ...

Click! Snap! Click! A stranger with an expensive camera hosting a huge lens stuck it in White Feather's face and started snapping pictures ... first landscape, then portrait, then from the side. With the quickness and ease of a man swatting a fly, White Feather snatched the camera away from the intruder leaving him gasping in shock. Ralph laughed while the other friends looked on with wide eyes perhaps fearing for the stranger's life.

The head chef, Birdie Beaudreau, raced up and pulled the skinny man away from White Feather's reach while scolding him. "What are you doin', fool?"

The weird little man answered in a strange accent, "Taking ze pictures."

"Well, you best take ze pictures somewhere else if'n you knows what's good for you."

As she dragged him away, he fought and reached for his camera. White Feather cradled the camera in his lap and continued eating calmly ignoring the rude man. Frank exclaimed, "What was that?"

Ralph had recovered and expressed his opinion as he scooped up corn on his fork. "Birdie called him "fool." Sounds about right."

Frank watched Birdie give the nervous man a proper dressing down before releasing him, then waddled back into the kitchen shaking her head in disgust. The man glanced around the room and then marched back over to White Feather. "Pardone, you have mine camera, senior."

White Feather slowly put down his fork and turned as if in slow motion to give the man a penetrating look.

"Ze face is of an Indian, no?"

White Feather turned back to his plate. "Cherokee."

The man's face lit up. "Like ze Will Rogers, yes?"

"Don't know any rope tricks."

"Read ze newspapers?"

"Don't learn anything from 'em."

"Perhaps, you could return mine camera?"

"Sit down." White Feather commanded calmly.

Frank pulled back a chair for him. The man dropped down obediently.

"Who are you?" White Feather demanded.

"O-Oh. M-My name is ..." he sat up straight and proudly declared, "Harold Flambeau!"

White Feather could not hold back a short chuckle. He handed the camera to the man with a warning. "No pictures."

Harold grabbed the camera and pulled it to his chest nodding his head. "Yes, yes, no pictures, no, no."

Albert attempted to break the tension. "Mr, Flambeau, are you here to photograph St. Jude?"

Harold draped the camera strap over his shoulder. "I am ze new resident of this beautimous releec."

Ralph wanted clarification. "You live here now?"

"Oh, yes, and most delightedly."

Frank asked, "Where are you from? I don't recognize your accent."

"Parees, of course."

"Paris, France?"

"Parees, Tex-as, mon ami."

Ralph choked. "Texas?"

"I am ze world famous photographer, you see."

The Wilsons entered the dining room. Mr. Wilson's dementia was most apparent as Mrs. Wilson led him across the room. Harold instinctively raised his camera to snap some photos. Again, White Feather snatched the camera away giving Flambeau's shoulder a jerk.

"Oh! No pictures! Yes, yes, no, no."

"Get food. Eat!" White Feather insisted as he once again placed Flambeau's camera in his lap. The frail man glanced around looking in the direction of the food trays and drinks.

Frank placed his napkin on the table. "Come on, I'll show you."

He led Flambeau to the carts and showed him how to retrieve a tray and get a drink. While away Ralph summed up his analysis of Flambeau. "Fruit cake."

The others at the table chuckled. Albert mused, "He is definitely a strange man. He appears to combine French, German, and English words interchangeably."

Ralph added, "Fake."

Albert said, "It would appear so, Rudolph."

Frank and Flambeau returned. The "Fake Fruit Cake" was laughing and chattering with Frank until he got close to White Feather. He eyed the Indian and then his camera. White Feather pointed at the empty chair and motioned with his finger to sit. Flambeau obeyed and was silent for the rest of the meal. This time, White Feather held on to the camera while Flambeau ate. Afterward, White Feather slung the camera over his shoulder and strolled out of the dining room with Harold following him like a young child being led to punishment.

Chapter 12

Sam Awakens

THE ALARM WOKE SAM Morrison only a few hours after he had finally managed to drop off to sleep. He turned onto his back and tried to force his eyes to focus on the ceiling light fixture. Undersheriff Crab had scheduled a meeting for 4:30 p.m. The raids would be reviewed and new assignments discussed. Sam glanced at the clock. It was 3:31 p.m. Still plenty of time, but he could not allow himself to go back to sleep.

The fog of waking in the middle of REM sleep made him crave returning to finish the sequence, so he threw off the covers hoping the chill would stimulate him. He rubbed his eyes with his palms as his mind returned to the subject that had prevented him from going to sleep for hours after he turned in. It was not the raid. The raid had gone smoothly since no one was at the house when they arrived. What kept him awake was what he had overheard while talking to Samantha. "Mom, he's here."

Who? Who had Samantha met? He had not seen her with anyone or heard anything. In such a small town, secrets could not be kept for long. Someone would have noticed. But, maybe that someone had kept it from him knowing it would be painful for him.

He had spent hours going over it in his head. How could he find out? Could he ask Tammy? No, she was too protective of her mother. Maybe he could ask Jerry? No, Jerry would just be disgusted with him. He should have done a drive by. No, Samantha would have been furious if she had seen him.

He should not be so possessive. He had lost that right. They were divorced and Samantha had every right to date someone else. But it was just too painful to think about.

Forcing himself out of bed, Sam headed for the shower. Maybe the answer would come to him in the shower. It often did, especially when working on a case. Something about the hot flowing water prompted clear thinking.

It did not work. His mind was too sluggish from lack of sleep. He almost dozed off in the shower. Sam finished shaving and brushing his teeth and hair and got dressed. He checked his watch. It was 3:48 p.m. It only took about three minutes to drive to work. He dragged himself downstairs to the kitchen, opened the refrigerator door and leaned in to let the frigid air cool his face.

His eyes did not want to focus on the shelves or search for something eatable. He realized that there was not that much to choose from, and he was not in the mood to cook. He grabbed the baloney and mayonnaise and closed the refrigerator.

He pulled out a couple of slices of white bread and grabbed a knife to spread the mayonnaise. He tore off a paper towel and placed it on the bar. He preferred to stand eating this time. He went back to the refrigerator for milk and poured half a glass. He needed to save some for later. He did not want to bother with the grocery store today.

He clicked on the television and watched cable news while he gulped the milk and ate the sandwich. There was only a brief mention of the nationwide raids on illegal grow sites. The valley was not mentioned. The clock over the fireplace showed 4:01 p.m. What the heck, he would just go in early.

It made no sense, but he swung by Samantha's house. She was, of course, at work, and Tammy and Jerry would still be at school. Now 4:06 p.m., he turned onto Bassick Street and passed by Samantha's office. Her car was in the parking lot. She was there. Life goes on.

He pulled into the parking lot at the sheriff's office at 4:09 p.m. The office was empty so he trudged into the breakroom to start the coffee. He sat down at the big work table and the next thing he knew, Undersheriff Crab was shaking him. "We keeping you awake, Deputy?"

Chapter 13

Taunting Flambeau

After lunch, Frank had retired to his room to watch television and relax. He was soon napping.

A knock on his door woke him. The sun was shining in his face through the window. He felt like he was being fried like a steak on a grill. In his old room, he could only tell the time with a clock. Now, he would have the window to keep him apprised of the day or night. What a huge difference it would make.

"Come in," he yelled as he struggled to climb out of the soft recliner so he could close the window blinds. The door swung open revealing Albert holding a bottle of wine in one hand and wine glasses in the other. "Welcome to your new home, Franklin!" Albert declared. Monty was giggling at Albert's side. And across the hall, the door opened and White Feather strolled out to join them. Frank grabbed the wine glasses and waved his friends inside. Albert expertly opened the wine as Monty found a spot on the bed to sit and White Feather claimed a corner of the room to stand with his arms crossed. Albert poured and Frank served as the old friends chattered happily and bragged on the new room.

Ralph appeared at the door to protest. "What're you guys doing in here?"

"Come in, Ralph. We are celebrating Franklin's new digs."

"Bring the party over to my place, more room."

They laughed and followed Ralph back to the rec room to gather around the card table. Ralph was noticeably proud of his arrangement and his friends had to admit that it would make a nice area to hang out. "I'm working on getting a pool table," Ralph proclaimed.

Albert inquired, "Where is Mr. Flambeau, White Feather?"

Ralph added, "You scalp him?"

White Feather ignored Ralph's remark. "Sulking."

"You give him back his camera?"

"Not yet."

The discussion turned to resident longevity. Frank asked, "Who has been here the longest?"

Albert glanced around, "I think that would be Walter and me. We've been here for over three years now."

He looked at Ralph, "Rudolph, you came not long after that followed by White Feather and finally Frank last year."

"Anyone here before you, Albert?"

"Oh, yes, I believe that Ruth moved in shortly after it was opened."

"When was that?"

Monty proclaimed, "January 1st, 2005."

That caught everyone's attention. Albert exclaimed, "Really? I did not know that Walter. Good to know."

Walter giggled and twiddled his fingertips together. "You mean I'm right?"

Even Ralph found his remark hilarious.

Albert added, "At first, everyone was given a room with an outside window. Then they had to start putting people in the inside rooms."

Frank asked, "Has St. Jude ever been full?"

"Oh, no, not even close. Residents are passing away almost as fast as new residents check in. The closest it has come to capacity was when you moved in, Frank."

"Lizzie had a nice room with that bay window."

"I think she and Ruth probably came to live here around the same time. They probably had their choice of rooms."

Frank looked at Ralph and shared, "Ralph asked for that room, but Barkley turned him down."

Ralph held out his hands. "Got a better deal."

All agreed. Monty asked, "Bu-but wh-why'd she t-turn you d-down on Elizabeth's old room?"

"Girl's room."

Frank explained, "She said that there is a rule against a man sharing a bathroom with a woman."

Ralph threw up his hands. "What are we . . . teenagers?"

Albert suggested, "I guess that makes sense. A woman doesn't want to have to deal with a slob in the bathroom."

"Hmmph. You should see their bathrooms."

They laughed and Frank challenged his friend asking, "When were you in one of their bathrooms?"

Ralph grumbled while his friends chided him.

Monty produced a deck of cards. "Texas Hold'em, anyone?"

Ralph waved him off, "Time for dinner."

Monty was undeterred. "Maybe we can steal some toothpicks to use for poker chips."

Frank remarked sarcastically, "Maybe Ralph's pool table will be here when we get back."

Hiiiiiii

The Sleuthkateers routinely gathered up their trays and drinks and sat down at their usual table without comment.

Timidly, the new resident, Harold Flambeau, slinked over to the table. Frank pulled back the chair next to White Feather for him. Flambeau sat down and tried to be nonchalant when he tilted his head over to check White Feather's lap for his camera.

"Will I ever get ze camera back?" he asked.

White Feather ignored him. Frank felt sorry for him. "Are you always taking pictures?"

"Oh, wee, monsieur. It is my passion."

Ralph chimed in, "Like scalping is the Injun's passion."

Flambeau covered his mouth and gasped, "Oh! Scalping?"

White Feather looked at Flambeau with wild eyes and slowly pulled out his Bowie knife and held it up for him to observe. Even the Sleuthkateers gasped at his audacity and then burst out laughing. Flambeau was visibly shaking as White Feather used the huge knife to cut his steak, stab the knife tip into a piece of steak and poke it into his mouth. Then he scooped up mashed potatoes with the knife and licked it off ravenously.

White Feather stared into Flambeau's eyes hypnotically as he wiped the knife on Flambeau's pants to clean it and then replaced it in its leather scabbard. Flambeau glanced around to each Sleuthkateer desperately seeking understanding. They were just holding their stomachs in laughter. "Eet is ze joke, no?"

Even White Feather chuckled.

Ralph shoveled mash potatoes into his mouth with his dinner knife and sneared. "Better check your scalp, paleface."

Flambeau reflexively grabbed the top of his head and stared at White Feather. The Indian had resumed eating and ignored the silly paleface.

Frank patted Flambeau on the back. "Relax, pardner. Eat your dinner."

The old friends laughed and joked with their new acquaintance well after dinner but were too tired to play Texas Hold'em afterward. As they were leaving the dining room, Frank watched White Feather ignore Flambeau. The poor man was too scared to bother him. They all retired to their separate rooms. Frank was glad. He was anxious to enjoy his second night in his new room.

Chapter 14

End of the Day

Frank heard a soft knocking on the door across the hallway. He shuffled quietly to his door to peek out. Harold Flambeau tentatively knocked on White Feather's door again. When there was no answer, he dropped his head, turned and walked away. As he reached the end of the hallway, White Feather bounded around the corner and stopped short of running over the newcomer.

"Oh!" shrieked Flambeau covering his head with his arms. White Feather stood with his arms crossed waiting.

"I come for ze camera."

White Feather responded by continuing down the hallway to his room. He walked in leaving the door open as an invitation for Flambeau to follow. Flambeau ventured up like a little boy afraid of what was awaiting him inside. Frank cracked open his door and mouthed quietly, "Go in," and nodded his head toward White Feather's room.

Flambeau inched that way and White Feather met him at the door. He handed Flambeau the camera and commanded, "We ride train tomorrow. Bring camera."

"Ze train? Vat train?"

"Royal Gorge Express."

"Why vee do dat?"

"You take pictures. Be in reception at 8:00 a.m."

"Ze breakfast?"

"Skipping. Be there."

With that, White Feather ushered him out the door and shut it with finality. Flambeau was flustered as he rushed off down the hallway. Frank could hear mysterious clicking sounds coming from White Feather's room. He tiptoed over and put his ear to the door. It sounded like typing.

Frank took a light step back and the old floor creaked loudly. Frank froze. The clicking sounds continued. Frank hustled back to his room and closed his squeaky door quickly. He placed his ear to his door to listen. It was silent outside his door. He walked over to his window, opened the shade and stared out at the subtle silhouette of the mountains against the dark sky. A star was shining brightly above the horizon . . . perhaps a planet. Frank dropped down into his recliner.

So White Feather would be joining the sheriff on the train. That was curious. The sheriff did suggest he ride the Royal Gorge Express sometime, but evidently White Feather had taken it as an invitation, not a suggestion. Frank chuckled to himself.

The really curious part was inviting Flambeau to go with him. What an odd couple. They have nothing in common and clearly White Feather detests Flambeau taking his picture. Frank closed his eyes and admitted to himself that if he ever got to the point of understanding White Feather then he was probably not of this world anymore.

Sean Bailey dragged himself into his house late that night. It had been a long, busy day. He had risen at 2:00 a.m. to get to the office and get his crew organized. Initially the raid had gone lightning fast, but then the wrapping up part took hours. There had been a lot of things to do to get paperwork finished and new assignments organized with the undersheriff.

There had been a ton of items on his to-do list and meetings. And just as he was straightening papers on his desk and stacking them neatly in separate project piles, the receptionist buzzed him. "Mark Doss from *The Chronicle* is here."

"Crap!" Sean whispered under his breath. He checked his watch. He had been putting him off all day, but now it was 5:30 p.m. "Okay, Gabby, send him back."

Sean took off his cap and placed it on the corner of his desk and sat back. In his head he began rehearsing what news he could give his friend about the raids. He got up and stepped next door to the undersheriff's office. "Attorney general send a press release yet?"

Buster was facing away working on something on the desk behind his main desk. He spun around. "Nope. I just checked a minute ago. Probably won't get it before tomorrow now."

"Okay. Thanks, Buster."

Doss turned the corner and spotted the sheriff. "Evening, Sean."

"Come in, Mark. Have a seat."

Mark Doss had been in his office many times and adjusted

his favorite chair near the window before sitting. He clicked on his pocket recorder and set it on Sean's desk. "You've had a long day."

Sean smiled. "Started at three this morning."

Mark shook his head, "Wow. Sounds like it was quite an operation."

"Yeah. There were raids across the nation besides our operation."

"So I hear. It go down smoothly?"

"For the most part it did. Three Cubans from one of the sites escaped and we are still searching for them. We think they headed north."

"Headed for Canon City?"

"Maybe. Possibly Salida. May double-back to Pueblo. We think they have connections down there." Sean waved his hands over his desk. "I'm sorry I don't have a press release yet. That'll come from the U. S. Attorney's Office . . . hopefully tomorrow."

Doss put down his pencil. "What can you give me today?"

Sean rolled his eyes. "Not too much. It was a joint task force of federal, state, and local law enforcement officials including Colorado Sheriff's SWAT teams, the Pueblo SWAT team, U.S. Drug Enforcement agents, all of Wet Mountain Valley deputy roster and posse members. We hit three sites in Wet Mountain Valley and five in Fremont County. I can't give you a figure on how many were arrested."

Sean rubbed his face with his palms. Mark took the hint. "This should get us started, Sean. I know you need to get home and rest. We did a lot of interviews of neighbors and looky-lous. We should be able to get something online tonight."

"Thanks, Mark. I will be out of pocket tomorrow, but Buster can keep you updated."

"I'll need a description of the fugitives."

Sean looked up to the ceiling and then back at Mark Doss. "Buster has that. I'll have him give you a copy."

"Okay, then." Mark leaned forward. "You going somewhere on business tomorrow?"

Sean had leaned forward but then sat back. "No. Pennie and I are going to Canon City to ride the Royal Gorge Express. We've had it planned for a while. A little R and R for us."

Mark stood and smiled. "Great. You should take some time off every now and then. I'll bug Buster tomorrow if we need anything."

Sean stood and shook the editor's hand. "Buster should have the press release for you tomorrow."

⸬⸬⸬⸬⸬⸬⸬⸬

Pennie was watching TV when Sean entered the living room. She looked at her watch. "You're running late. Did the big raid go well?"

Sean dropped onto the couch and pulled off his boots. "Went well except for three Cubans who managed to slip off."

Pennie's eyes got big. Sean knew what she was thinking. "Don't worry, we're still a go for tomorrow."

Pennie relaxed slightly and then started to ask, but Sean headed her off. "Buster will handle it. I won't have to be involved."

Pennie gave him a sideways look. Sean raised his hands. "Honest."

Pennie stood and headed for the kitchen. "Have you eaten anything?"

Sean pulled off his gun belt and moved to his recliner. "No. Too busy. Not that hungry though so don't go to any trouble."

Pennie ignored his comment. "It made the channel six news. They didn't say anything about the Cubans. They just talked about the helicopter and armored vehicles and interviewed a lot of neighbors. We know all of them ... the usual suspects."

Pennie loaded a tray and headed back to the living room. She found Sean sleeping.

PART III:

[Wednesday] Royal Gorge Express

Chapter 15

Who's on First Base?

T HE DIRECT RAYS FROM the morning sun made the snow-capped Sangre de Christo Mountains sparkle while puffy but shadowy, subdued clouds perched over them. The dining room mood was gloomy matching the heavily filtered light from outside.

Ralph Jacobs had been focused on his meal. Albert Stein sat thoughtfully engaged with his newspaper. Walter Montgomery had paused to study the curious newcomer sitting alone in the corner. Frank Roberts chewed on a crunchy English muffin and wiped butter from the corner of his mouth. Ralph loaded his mouth with a slice of biscuit dripping with cream gravy, glanced at the empty chair at their table and asked, "Where's the Injun?"

Frank replied, "White Feather has gone to ride the Royal Gorge Express today."

"What's that?" Ralph asked.

"The train over in Canon City."

Ralph swallowed and reloaded with bacon. "Where's he going?"

"Well, to ride the train, as I said."

"Where?"

Albert got it. "It doesn't go anywhere, Rudolph, just up through the Royal Gorge canyon and then back to Canon City."

Ralph paused and stared at Albert. "Why? They forget something?"

Frank was exasperated. Albert resumed reading. Walter asked, "Why do you think he's so sullen?"

Ralph bit off a piece of bacon and sliced off more biscuit and gravy with the edge of his fork. "Probably because he didn't get nowhere."

Walter looked at Ralph bewildered. Frank glanced over at the newcomer in the corner and thought Walter was right. The elderly man looked sullen and defiant sitting all alone. "What do you know about him, Albert?"

Ralph stuffed the dripping bite in his mouth. "Yeah, he gonna stay on or get off?"

Albert closed and folded the paper and set it beside his plate. "Not much. Birdie thinks he may have been the sheriff in Wet Mountain Valley years ago."

Ralph reached for his glass of orange juice. "Not likely them ranchers would let an Injun sheriff 'em."

Walter frowned. "Injun? You think he's Native American?"

Ralph managed to say "Duh!" before placing the glass to his lips.

Frank commented, "Doesn't look Native American, does he?"

Albert chuckled and then looked directly at Ralph and smiled. "It seems you gentlemen are not on the same page."

Ralph set down his orange juice, "Duh!"

Albert continued, "We're talking about the new resident sitting alone over there, Rudolph. You are still hung up on White Feather."

Ralph jerked his head around. "I thought you said he was in Canon City?"

Frank was frustrated. "White Feather IS in Canon City. We're not talking about White Feather!"

"He ain't ridin' that train?" asked Ralph.

Frank, Walter and Albert looked at each other and then burst out laughing. Ralph glared at them, threw down his fork and stormed out of the dining room.

"Ralph!" Walter pleaded, "Wh-What's wrong?!"

Albert touched Walter's arm, "Let it be, Walter. He'll calm down. We can straighten things out when we join him in the pool room."

"It's a shame," Frank said.

"Wh-What is?" asked Walter.

"Ralph is the one among us that has the guts to approach this new guy and find out about him."

They nodded their heads in agreement. Then Frank remembered the other new person at St. Jude."We shouldn't forget about the other new resident . . . Harold Flambeau! Poor White Feather. He's stuck on the train with him today."

Albert asked in surprise, "White Feather took Mr. Flambeau with him?"

"Yeah," Frank answered. "Overheard him tell Flambeau to be in the lobby by 8:00 a.m. and bring his camera."

Walter interjected, "I th-thought he t-took his camera."

Frank explained, "I saw White Feather give it back last night."

Walter was curious. "Wh-Why the interest in th-the t-train?"

Frank shrugged.

Albert proposed, "Let's go check out the new guy . . . introduce ourselves.

The man seemed unaware of their approach until Albert reached out his hand. "Good morning, I'm Albert Stein and these are my friends Walter Montgomery and Franklin Roberts."

The man squeezed their hands a little too firmly and did not offer his name or any sort of greeting.

"We just want to welcome you to St. Jude."

He still gave no response.

"May we join you?"

He motioned for them to sit but was not welcoming. Monty tried to start the conversation by asking, "Wh-What b-brings you t-to St. Jude?"

Frank and Albert winced and the man's glare suggested he agreed that it was an improper question. Everyone at St. Jude was there because they had no other option. It was a home for the indigent.

Now Albert tried by asking, "Are you from the Wet Mountain Valley?"

The man shrugged, "Yeah, you?"

"Monty is; I came here from Denver; Frank via Canon City."

The large man leaned back, took a deep breath and began his story. "Moved to the valley in 1945. Worked on a ranch and later leased a place of my own. Was sheriff for ten years until I got shot in the shoulder." He rubbed his left shoulder.

Albert commented, "I think we've met. I may have interviewed you when I was researching a story. I was a reporter for *The Denver Post*."

"Yeah, maybe. I was interviewed pretty often about one thing or another. Part of the job."

Frank asked, "You play pool? We were about to go up for a game or two."

The sullen man tilted his head to one side. "Why not."

As they left the dining room, Mrs. Barkley approached. "Good morning, gentlemen. I see you've met Mr. Slade."

Albert admitted, "Well, we haven't been formally introduced."

"Oh, well, Cody Slade, this is Albert Stein, Walter Montgomery, and Frank Roberts."

The men remained aloof, understandably choosing not to shake this man's hand again. Moving on from a slightly awkward moment, Mrs. Barkley addressed Frank, "How is your room, Frank?"

"Great! Oh, but I need help turning on the little refrigerator."

"I'll have TJ stop by."

"You have a refrigerator in your room?" Slade asked.

Frank shrugged shyly. "I just moved into a new room. It has a small apartment-style refrigerator but it is turned off. I thought it might be nice to store a carton of milk in it."

Slade frowned. "Milk? Ya' need beer if you ask me."

Frank was embarrassed. He was relieved when the elevator doors opened.

Chapter 16

Cody Slade and the Pool Game

Albert handled introductions. "Rudolph, this is Cody Slade, a new resident. We invited him to join us for a pool match."

Slade reached out his hand and Frank wanted to warn Ralph, but it was too late. Stubbornly, Ralph accepted the challenge and appeared to be trying to crank down on Slade's grip. Slade mercifully released when Ralph's face turned bright red.

Ralph was still angry with his friends, but put it aside. He was always in the mood for pool. "Me 'n him'll take Frank 'n Monty."

Albert smiled kindly at Slade. "Okay with you, Mr. Slade?"

Slade shrugged, retrieved a pool cue and chalked the tip rigorously. Ralph had already racked the balls so he placed the cue ball on the table and took out all his anger on the break. The balls exploded and bounced around the table. A striped ball dropped into the corner pocket. Ralph rechalked his cue tip and leaned over for his next shot.

Slade asked, "You fellows lived here long?"

Ralph pulled back his cue and turned to glare at the newcomer. Albert interceded. "Ralph does not like for us to talk while he is taking a shot."

Slade glared back at Ralph. "Sorry, go ahead."

Ralph leaned over again to resume play. He pulled the cue stick back and rocked it back and forth several times before making his shot, while at the same moment Frank chose to answer Slade's question. "I've only been here about a year."

Ralph lunged forward striking the cue ball off center sending it spinning into the side pocket. Ralph exploded into a tirade of expletives and started swinging his cue stick like a baseball bat with apparent intent of beheading Frank.

With lightening fast reflexes, Slade grabbed the cue stick and jerked it away from Ralph leaving the angry man and spectators in shock.

"There's no need for violence, gentlemen." The ex-sheriff proclaimed calmly.

Monty pulled the cue ball out of the pocket and suggested Ralph replay the shot. Slade handed back the cue stick and gestured with his head toward the table. Ralph replayed the shot but missed slightly leaving the target ball in front of the pocket.

Monty stepped up to take his turn while Ralph quizzed the new guy. "Who are you?"

Albert replied, "Mr. Slade was once the sheriff of Wet Mountain Valley."

Slade added, "Among other things."

Monty did not pocket a ball, so Slade stepped up to the table.

"Like what?" Ralph persisted.

"Ranching mostly. What'd you do in your previous life?"

He aimed at the cue ball and sent it zinging across the table to knock in the green fourteen ball. The cue ball banked and rolled back to line up on the nine ball.

"Construction engineer."

Slade popped the nine into the side pocket putting backup on the cue ball to line up on the fifteen in the corner. Now the old men got quiet to watch Slade run the table putting Ralph into a joyous and triumphant mood. Slade became his temporary best friend.

Ralph asked, "You know about that big raid?"

Slade squinted. "What do you know about it?"

"Three cartel hoodlums got away. I saw 'em in our kitchen last night."

Slade was interested. "In the kitchen downstairs here?"

"Yep. I was down there ..." He paused to glance at his friends and then continued in a more confidential tone, "I was hungry and went down to raid the icebox. I heard something and saw two of 'em by the drink carts and then heard the other one in the kitchen fumbling around."

Slade cocked his head to one side. "You must be Jacobs' old man."

Albert corrected him. "Grandfather. Rudolph is Deputy Jacobs' grandfather."

Slade sized up Ralph. "What'd you do?"

Ralph was confused. "Raised her old man."

Slade broke into his first smile. "I mean in the kitchen."

"Got a couple of tuna fish sandwiches and returned to my room."

Albert, Monty, and Frank could not help laughing, but Slade gave him a look that said he was not convinced. Ralph must have realized how unbelievable his story was, so he voluntarily explained, "I was in Korea and have been diagnosed with PSTEDQRST so I thought I was just having one my spells."

"PSTEDQRST?"

Ralph got defensive. "Whatever they call shell shock these days."

Slade said, "Oh, PTSD."

"So, anyways, I thought I was reliving an episode from the war. But when Sydney told me about the raid, I realized it was real."

Slade was getting impatient. "Sydney one of your imaginary friends?"

"Sydney is my granddaughter. She's a deputy for this county."

Slade raised an eyebrow. "Right, Deputy Jacobs."

"Yeah, she comes by to see me all the time. She came by after the raid."

"So, you think they may still be here?"

Frank answered, "I saw them up on Cemetery Hill yesterday morning. White Feather and I checked it out and they were headed north."

"How do you know that?"

"White Feather is an Indian and he read their tracks."

Slade shook his head. "You guys are real jokesters aren't you. You must think I fell off a turnip wagon."

This clearly raised Frank and Ralph's dander. Albert stepped in to try to save the peace. "As strange as it may seem,

Mr. Slade, I must say that these two are not trying to pull your leg. Rudolph did serve in Korea and his granddaughter is Deputy Jacobs. And I did see her here yesterday morning too. White Feather is a resident of St. Jude and was a Cherokee medicine man in his younger days."

Slade studied Albert thinking his demeanor seemed quite refined and intellectual. And Albert detected that Cody was still not convinced. Albert was also curious about Cody's interest in their stories. "You seem to be very interested in the fugitives?"

Slade turned back to Frank. "I would like to see those tracks."

Frank shrugged, "Sure. Come with me."

Frank's muscles were still sore from climbing Cemetery Hill the previous day. Slade and Albert strode up the hill with no problem, while Ralph and Monty fell behind.

Slade knelt down to examine the indentions just as White Feather had done. He also found the tracks leading north out of the glen. "Headed north all right."

Ralph trudged up and found an old stump to sit on and said, "Everbody knows they went north. Got an APB out on 'em."

Slade looked perturbed. "You get that from Jacobs too?"

"Nope. Channel six news this morning."

Chapter 17

Dead Man at Lost Trail Ranch

Deputy Sam Morrison heard the call while driving into the office. "Body found at Lost Trail Ranch."

He knew that he would be assigned anyway, so he reported in, turned on the lights, and headed directly for the Lost Trail Ranch ten miles north of Rockcliffe. The ranch foreman had reported a dead body by the tractor barn and a missing pickup truck.

Although it was a significant lead, he had driven Highway 69 many times before and it wasn't his first homicide, so his mind wandered to his family shortly after passing Copper Gulch Road. After fretting over his wife for two days, either his mind had worked it out or just gotten tired of the agony.

Today he found himself in a mood to re-engage and fight for her again. But at that moment, he had a bad feeling about his son, Jerry. Samantha was also very concerned about Jerry. He was becoming lethargic, lazy, and his grades were suffering. Morrison was worried that it might be drugs but had not mentioned his suspicions to Samantha.

He and Samantha had been getting along quite well during the winter with plenty of school events providing excuses to be with her. But now things had slowed down and he felt that he was losing ground. He began trying to think of an excuse to call her. Maybe he could plan an outing with Jerry … and Tammy.

Samantha had moved herself and the kids to Rockcliffe and filed for divorce after he had neglected her and the kids because of his job with the Denver P.D. Samantha had not disguised her contempt for him following them to Rockcliffe to accept a job as deputy.

He still could not believe he let things get to this point. She had given him every opportunity to reconcile, but he had been too dumb to recognize them. At this point, he was not sure he could ever get back into her good graces. It had taken a lot of work just to regain her friendship.

The gate for the Lost Trail Ranch appeared as he rounded a curve. Two tall lodge poles were set beside the cattle guard with another lodge pole across the top. "Lost Trail Ranch" was engraved on a wide sign attached to the top lodge pole.

Morrison slowed and turned onto the gravel road that led off west and then curved around behind a forested hill. The ranch bordered the St. Jude Methodist Retirement Center on the north. It was a 2,000 acre cattle ranch owned by one of the valley's prominent ranching families.

The ranch foreman's pickup was stopped by the side of the road waiting. Morrison pulled up alongside and rolled down the passenger side window. The rugged foreman acknowledged him. "Mornin' Deputy. I'll take you to the barn."

"Mornin'. Thanks."

Morrison followed the foreman down a rutted road to a large barn surrounded by hay equipment and a pole barn filled with hay bales. The foreman stopped in front of the tall, double doors of the tractor barn, got out and pointed to the side of the barn.

Morrison only needed a glance at the body to know that it was one of the cartel fugitives. He was a young Latino wearing camouflage shirt and pants. He was still clutching his AK47 assault rifle. His body was riddled with bullet holes and he was lying in a muddy puddle of blood.

The foreman walked up beside Morrison and explained, "We found him early this morning. The pickup we had parked inside the barn is missing."

Morrison took out his notepad. "Can you describe the truck?"

"Black 2008 Dodge Ram 1500 SLT with the double cab."

"License number?"

The foreman reached into his shirt pocket and pulled out a crumpled piece of paper, unfolded it, and handed it to Morrison. The license number was scribbled in bold letters with a long number below it. The Foreman explained, "VIN number."

"Thanks. Perfect." Morrison wrote down the license number in his notepad and stuffed the note in his shirt pocket. "Any idea when this went down?"

"Nah. Nobody's been out here for several days."

"You find the body?"

"Yeah. I came over to pick up some wire to fix the fence." He pointed west.

Morrison handed him his card. "Thanks. I'll call it in. Al will come out ..."

The foreman frowned. Morrison explained, "Al, the coroner, will come out and tape it off. Need to keep people away from the scene. The CBI will probably send out a team as well."

"I'll keep an eye on it. Shouldn't be anybody around here anyway."

The foreman drove away as Morrison tried to trace the tracks of the pickup coming out of the barn. Looked like the truck had been driven out through the main gate. It was anyone's guess where the driver took the vehicle from there.

Morrison was sure it was one of the cartel fugitives but hesitated to report it to the CBI. He did not want to deal with Agent S. Miles Blakeley. Maybe he would check around to see if anyone else had seen anything first.

He drove back to highway 69 and headed north. After five miles, he realized that there were no houses right on the highway in that area. Finally, a small house with a decaying wood barn appeared.

He pulled into the driveway and parked next to a 1968 Ford pickup that didn't look as though it had been moved in years. Weeds had grown up around the truck. He knocked on the door and waited. Knocked again and waited. After four tries the weathered door was pulled open. An old man leaning on an aluminum walker stood next to the door. "Yeah?"

Morrison took out a card, opened the screen door and handed it to the old man. "I'm Deputy Morrison with the Wet Mountain Sheriff's Office. I was wondering if you noticed a black 2008 Dodge Ram 1500 SLT with a double cab go by yesterday about this time?"

The old man spit and started pushing the door closed. Morrison stuck his foot in to stop the door from closing. "Sir, did you see ...."

"Psst, I never look at the damn road. Too much traffic."

Morrison let him close the door. He felt a little silly. Why would anyone along the road pay any attention to the cars passing by? He went back to his SUV and radioed in asking Gabby to report the incident to the CBI.

Chapter 18

Arrival of Sean and Pennie

"We're here yet," Sean announced as he pulled his pickup into a parking spot. It had been a long, somber drive from their home near Rockcliffe, Colorado, down through the Wet Mountain Valley on the Oak Creek Grade to Canon City. Neither had been in the mood to talk. Pennie retrieved her purse from the floor board.

Sean climbed out and waited for Pennie so he could lock the doors. He guessed the temperature to be ten to fifteen degrees hotter here in the arid valley of Canon City at 5,333 feet above sea level. That put it 2,500 feet below Rockcliffe at 7,888. It reminded him of the days when he worked as a police officer in this hotter climate before being elected Wet Mountain Valley sheriff and moving up to Rockcliffe.

The shutting of the passenger door startled Sean. He took a deep breath. He reminded himself that he was not on duty today. Wet Mountain Valley and the sheriff's office could survive without him for one day. He checked his bare hip where his gun would normally be. He checked his chest where his badge would normally be, then his pocket where he had stashed it--just in case. But today he was a civilian, not the Wet Mountain Valley Sheriff.

Sean locked the truck and closed the driver's door. As they ambled across the parking lot toward the train terminal, Sean began doubting the wisdom of this venture. They had both been in a funk after their youngest son, Randy, had recently deployed to Afghanistan with his marine unit. They had been through it several times with their oldest, but he was in the Navy and it somehow seemed different than being on the ground. So, Sean had enthusiastically suggested the outing to Pennie and she had seemed to like the idea.

Sean looked over at the long passenger train. The orange and yellow engines were only partially visible behind an antique steam engine sitting on a separate track beside them. Attached to the engines were two blue trimmed cars with tall, domed roofs the website had called the "Vista Domes." One would be "First Class" serving a "special dining experience" for the passengers.

Behind the Vista Domes was a "Club Class" car with tables and a bar, followed by a "Coach Class" car with high-backed, soft lounger-style seating, followed by an open car where passengers could walk around and enjoy unobstructed views of the gorge followed by a long string of cars repeating the configuration at least three times over.

The Royal Gorge Express makes a two-hour trip up through the Royal Gorge and back several times a day in the summer. The deep, thin sliced gorge is a major Colorado attraction and Sean had scheduled them for the Club Class lunch train followed by a trip to the top of the gorge to see the Royal Gorge bridge.

It was a suspension bridge "to nowhere" 955 feet above the raging Arkansas River and railroad tracks below. The buildings on either side of the gorge had to be restored after a fire had destroyed them several years before. So they had decided to see what had changed since the last time they had visited the famous Colorado landmark.

As they walked along the side of the terminal, Sean spotted the enigmatic White Feather sitting in the shade with his arms folded and eyes closed. White Feather's trademark hair style tickled him. The top portion of his hair was threaded through a hollow deer leg bone so that it sprayed up like a shock of grass atop his head.

A single white feather danced in the breeze beside his face with the hilt tied to the deer bone. The back portion of his hair was braided and fell down to the center of his back. The old Cherokee elder was wearing a red plaid short-sleeved shirt, Levis and cowboy boots. He appeared to be valiantly trying to endure the heat or was he trying to endure the tall, skinny man with the camera snapping pictures of him?

Sean had first met White Feather during the Ludwig triple homicide investigation. At that time, White Feather was just an old vagabond living in an abandoned train terminal in Rockcliffe. White Feather had stumbled upon the Ludwig boy, David, who was their prime suspect in the case. Unbeknownst to anyone, David had suffered a brain injury in football practice. He had lost the ability to manage his memories the day of the homicide. When White Feather found the boy in the park, he had sensed David was innocent and had used his exotic skills as a Native American medicine man and priest to investigate and eventually help solve the case. Afterward, White Feather had moved into the St. Jude Methodist Retirement Home.

Snap, snap, snap. The loud, clicking noise caught Sean's attention. The tall, skinny man was snapping pictures of White Feather and jabbering incessantly commanding him to smile or look this way or that. Sean detected a strange accent that he could not quite place. White Feather waved his hand across his face as if shooing away a fly.

"Poor White Feather," Pennie whispered. Then the rude photographer turned his attention to them and started snapping their picture. When Sean started to reach out to block the offensive photographer, Pennie nudged him away. "Don't forget, you're off today."

"Good morning, White Feather, everything okay here?"

White Feather nodded and grunted, "Morning, Sheriff."

Sean and Pennie went into the terminal and while Sean lined up at the ticket counter, Pennie roamed around in the gift shop searching for treasures. There were already several long lines leading up to the ticket windows. Sean glanced around expecting to see someone he knew.

Becoming the sheriff of Wet Mountain Valley made him a local celebrity and he had become accustomed to greeting his friends and neighbors. He sometimes felt as if he were always campaigning for office. But this was not the Wet Mountain Valley and although only about fifty miles from home, the ticket line was filled with unfamiliar faces--tourists, he surmised.

"Snap." Sean was momentarily blinded by the flash of the thin man's camera. "Snap, snap." The man panned around the room shooting pictures of everyone and everything in the area.

"Hey!" One man yelled as others put their arms up to block the offensive flashes. The thin man ignored the protests and rushed into the gift shop to continue his documentary. Low, grumbling protests spread around the room. Sean shook his head. He was "off duty" and decided to let the incident go. He hoped that he would not have to break up a fight later, but he could see that the strange camera buff was offending people wherever he went and leaving unhappy people in his wake.

"I thought I'd find you here." A man in a khaki shirt that matched his pants said quietly in the next line. Sean glanced in time to see the man standing in front of him appear surprised and say, "What are you doing here?"

The man in khakis surreptitiously looked around before answering. Sean acted as if he were not interested. Khaki guy responded, "I came to keep an eye on my investment."

The comment seemed to rattle the young man dressed in white short pants with a blue, flowery shirt. Sean noticed his expensive Nike tennis shoes and "no show" socks, as Pennie referred to such socks.

"We're just getting away for the day. It's been planned for ..."

"Kind of an expensive getaway for a man who says he's broke."

Sean tried not to think the worst--a loan shark harassing a client. Of course, it could be anything. Perhaps a father-in-law? Or maybe a jealous neighbor?

Khaki guy gave the room the once over again and then strolled away. Blue flowers turned to watch him leave with nervous eyes. Now he could see the expensive chain necklaces draped around his neck. He was a vain man with expensive tastes.

Sam Learns of Jerry's Arrest

Deputy Morrison's cell phone buzzed as he approached Copper Gulch Road returning to the office. A picture of the smiling face of Undersheriff Buster Crab was displayed. He opened up the call. "Hey, Buster, what's up?"

"Got bad news, Sam. Jerry was picked up in one of the raids."

"Jerry? My son?"

"Yeah. They got him over in Canon City."

"Samantha know?"

"You're the only one I've told."

"Why was he picked up?"

"I guess he was working at one of the sites."

"Working?"

"I don't have any more than that right now, Sam."

Sam dropped the phone down. His mind was spinning. He raised the phone again. "I'm gonna need the day, Buster."

"I figured. Keep me posted."

Sam pulled into the park and ride parking at the intersection of Copper Gulch Road and Highway 69. Samantha would be devastated. He found her number in his phone and started to tap it, but hesitated. He decided he should tell her in person. He pulled back on to Highway 69, turned on the lights and floored the accelerator.

After the Credit Union had closed, Samantha had gone to work part-time at the bank and then landed a job with the title company that purchased the old credit union building. Sam found her working at her desk. He was out of breath as he plopped down into the guest chair. "Sam, there's … well … Jerry's been …"

Samantha grabbed her throat. "Jerry? What's happened to Jerry?"

Sam looked down. "He's been arrested."

Samantha gasped and clasped her hands over her mouth. Sam wanted to hug her but resisted. "I don't know the details. He was picked up in the raid. He's in Canon City."

"He's in jail?"

"Yes."

Samantha stood. "We've gotta get him out, Sam!"

"I'm headed there next. I've taken the day off."

Samantha grabbed her coat. "I'm going with you!"

Sam stood and looked around. "Do you need to tell someone?"

Samantha placed her hand on her forehead. "Crap."

She turned and stormed into one of the back offices. There was a brief, animated discussion with her boss and then she raced back out. "Let's go."

🛤

They barely closed the doors to his SUV when Samantha bombarded him with questions. "Why was he arrested?"

"All I know is that he was picked up in one of the raids."

"Raids?"

"I told you about the raids."

"Oh, yes, I guess you did."

"Joint Federal, State and local raids on illegal grow sites."

"What's a grow site?"

"Marijuana grow site. You know, where they ..."

"Oh, okay. Didn't know you called them that."

"Oh, dear!" Samantha broke down in tears and tried to speak through her sobs. "Jerry was supposed to be working over in Alamosa."

"Alamosa?"

"He told me he had a construction job over there and would be staying with the crew for several days."

Sam did not respond. He wanted to quiz her more, but could see that this was not the time.

"When were the raids?"

"Yesterday morning."

Samantha looked at her ex-husband with concern. "He's been in jail for two days? Why didn't you tell me?"

Sam raised his hands in defense. "I just heard about it! I came straight over after Buster called."

Samantha rubbed her forehead. "Weren't you there?"

"No, not at that site."

"Why didn't he call? Why didn't someone call us?"

It was a good question. Sam did not have an answer for her except to speculate. "Maybe he was embarrassed. It probably took a while for them to process everyone."

Sam looked at her with pleading eyes. "I'm sorry, Sam. We'll get him out. Everything will be okay."

Samantha shook her head and blew her nose, then took a deep breath, dropped her hands into her lap, sat back and looked out the windshield. "I should've checked on it. Jerry has been acting strangely lately. He stays out late. Always has some lame excuse. He blows up when I try to ask him about anything."

Sam started to tell her he had noticed the change in Jerry, but waited. Samantha continued, "I didn't want to believe that Jerry was doing drugs, but all the signs were there. I've failed him!"

"No! No, Sam, you couldn't have known for sure. Teenagers are moody and rebellious. Doesn't mean they're into drugs ... or anything."

She turned her sad, puppy-dog eyes on him. "Have you noticed anything?"

"Same thing as you. He's been lethargic, uninspired. I wanted to talk to you about it, but I wasn't sure. Jerry has always been kind of lazy or laid back. Nothing like Tammy. Opposites. But kids are different."

Samantha huffed. "I blame that Jones girl."

"Jones girl?"

"Jenny. The coach's daughter."

"Jerry still has a crush on her after all that happened?"

"She's a manipulator. Has everyone convinced she's off drugs ... into Jesus now."

"You don't believe her?"

Samantha tried to control her anger. "Oh, I don't know. I guess it's possible. She has Jerry wrapped around her little finger."

"They're dating?"

"Sort of, I guess. They go to church stuff together. He hangs out over at her place a lot."

Sam started thinking out loud. "Could be supplying him with drugs, or maybe hooking him up with dealers."

Samantha got quiet. Her eyes were drying out as she stared straight ahead. For once, thankfully, she was not critical of his speeding.

As they sat in silence, Sam remembered Jenny Jones from the Ludwig case. The investigation had turned up pictures of drug parties in one of the cabins on Lake DeWeese. One picture depicted Jenny in the middle of an apparent orgy with other kids looking on and cheering.

Sam was relieved when nothing in the investigation indicated that Jerry had been involved in any of the drug parties. However, he had been concerned that Jerry harbored a secret crush on her.

The investigation blew the town apart. So many kids had been involved and the parents and teachers were at a loss for what to do. Several of the churches got involved and there was a coordinated community effort to "save the kids."

Sam was sure that it mostly worked. Drug related crimes were down in the valley since then. He hoped that the cartels had not brought the problem back.

Chapter 20

Columbine Club's Arrival

Compared to getting twenty-four independent minded ladies together and organized, herding cats was easy. The clock was ticking and Lena, president of the exclusive ladies only Columbine Club, counted only four of the twenty-four Columbine Club members in the lobby of the Royal Gorge Express terminal. She was one and the other three made four of the five ladies that rode with her from Rockcliffe. Not only were the other ladies late, her group was shrinking.

"Where is Bessie?" Lena asked as she dug through her purse looking for the confirmation papers. Her three friends glanced around and shrugged. Elizabeth, the social butterfly of the club offered, "I guess she went to the ladies' room. Oh, look at these blouses, Lena, aren't they adorable?"

"There's Florence and her bunch," Theresa observed as she held her purse close to her heart and appeared to be disinterested in the gifts and souvenirs. She was the shrewd, quiet member.

"Where's everyone else?" Lena asked rhetorically.

Lena shook her head and got in line for tickets. "Let's all be fashionably late," she quipped to herself. She noticed Sean

Bailey, the Wet Mountain Sheriff at one of the ticket windows. She almost did not recognize him dressed casually instead of in his uniform. She glanced around the gift shop looking for Pennie. When she spotted her, she smiled to herself. It was nice to see that they might take a day off every now and again.

One by one, the esteemed members of the one hundred year old Wet Mountain Valley Columbine Club collected in the gift shop and joked, touched, handled, and tried on the huge collection of odd objects and clothes. Miraculously, with less than five minutes to spare, the rest of the club members, even Bessie, appeared.

Lena raised her hand and waved as she shouted, "Okay, ladies, we need to head down to gate number Two." She held up two fingers above her head. "Follow me."

As she marched out of the terminal, down the walkway and found the line for gate number two, the ladies sort of followed. A flash momentarily blinded her and a tall, lanky man with a hat pushing down curly black hair turned his camera to click others, the train and then rushed off to the next gate.

A tall, skinny, red-headed boy dressed in an ill-fitting white uniform and wearing a black conductor's hat announced, "This is the line for Vista Domes 1 and 2. If your ticket is not for Vista Dome 1 or 2, please come forward and I will direct you to the proper line. We will be boarding in five minutes."

A number of people pushed forward to show him their tickets. Lena looked up to find three club members waiting with their tickets in hand in front of the boy.

"Ladies! What are you doing?" Lena shouted.

"Checking in," one of them responded.

Exasperated, Lena replied, "You don't need to check in yet, get back in line."

"But he said ..."

"He said to come forward if you're ticket is NOT for Vista Dome 1 or 2. We are in Vista Dome 2."

The ladies squinted at their tickets turning them this way and that as they retreated back to the line.

⊞⊞⊞⊞

As Sean and Pennie left the terminal and headed for their gate, two middle-aged men were noisily arguing. They were angry, but grumbling more than yelling. One was hefty, probably 250 pounds, the other slightly taller but thinner at probably 200 pounds. The argument was escalating and Sean felt Pennie tug on his arm to lead him away and avoid the scuffle. "You're off today," she reminded him.

Sean smiled and avoided intervening as the two men began shoving each other. He hoped that Pennie was proud of him, because he really wanted to break up the fight.

He handed her a ticket and they paused in the line at gate 3. A teen-aged girl dressed in a black uniform turned her head to face into the breeze and swiped her long brown stringy hair out of her face. Sean checked his watch. Four minutes until their boarding time.

Pennie pointed toward gate two. "Oh, look, there's Maybell and Bessie. And there's Lena. It must be the Columbine Club."

"I thought we might see someone we know on the train."

Pennie seemed disappointed. "Yeah, we always run into someone we know."

Sean spotted White Feather at the front of their line but decided not to mention it.

Five minutes came and went. Some checked their watches or their cell phones. Some tapped on their watches and held them up to their ear to listen to them. The lanky red-head at gate 2 seemed completely oblivious to time or even where in the world he was currently standing. Lena supposed that the young man was probably deep in a daydream. The Columbine ladies were getting very restless.

A whistle blew drawing the young man out of his dream. He cheerfully announced, "Okay, time to board, show me your tickets."

Lena waved for the ladies to come forward. Three held their tickets above their heads and waved them to show them to the boy. Lena shook her head and instructed them to hand their tickets to him. Lena guided the rest of her fellow club members up to the young man and then herded them to the second oversized, blue domed car to board.

When they were at last on board, several of the ladies seeing the booths complained, "Where are the card tables?"

"We will be using the dining tables. You will just have to hold your cards at an angle. Now please be seated so we can start the meeting."

The ladies paired off, found opponents, and then found tables. Once settled, Lena addressed her friends. "Well, here we are. Our thanks to Elizabeth for suggesting this for our 100th anniversary party. What a clever idea."

The ladies applauded while Elizabeth feigned embarrassment. "As a special treat, I have asked Florence to put together the history of the club."

Florence pulled out several pages typed front and back from her purse and rushed to the center of the car. As she unfolded the pages, she began, "As you can guess, trying to condense one hundred years of history into a 'relatively' short talk is nearly impossible. We are fortunate to have minutes from January 1976 to the present. These minutes were a tremendous help in compiling this brief history. As with minutes of any group, the minutes reflect the personality of the Secretary. Some minutes were extensive and for a few years in the mid-nineties the minutes could only be called minimal, very minimal ..."

Chapter 21

Club Car

SEAN WAS PLEASANTLY SURPRISED by the Club car. It had what appeared to be a bar in the center with plenty of tables and chairs. Beautiful polished wood adorned the walls and ceiling of their car. Sean had chosen the Club Class car because it was not as expensive as the Vista Dome cars, but not the least expensive option either. Judging from the website pictures, he thought this car might not be as cramped. The chairs around the tables were not fixed to the floor.

He saw White Feather again, this time sitting alone by the window. He and Pennie stopped momentarily to be friendly. "Hello, White Feather."

Sean reached out to shake White Feather's hand. White Feather waved for them to join him. Sean glanced around and did not see anyone they knew. He knew Pennie would prefer to sit alone, but no matter where they sat, they would be joined by strangers, so he nudged Pennie to have a seat.

Pennie and White Feather sat across from each other in the window seats, while Sean sat in the aisle seat next to Pennie. The chair style enabled Sean to have plenty of needed leg room for his six foot six inch tall frame.

"Click, click, click."

The familiar sound of the irritating photographer caught his attention. The rude man was snapping pictures of everything inside the car. Sean glanced across to see White Feather ignoring the photographer. "Hey, fella, lose the camera," someone shouted.

The fella paid no attention as he rushed out of the car to the next one. A young man approached and handed them menus. "Welcome to the Royal Gorge Express, would you ..." he paused when he saw the extraordinary appearance of White Feather and then continued, "folks like something to drink?"

"We're moving!" Pennie noticed. Sean looked out the window and was surprised that he had not felt the train start moving. Pennie asked, "Do we eat now?"

The attendant smiled and held out his hands, "Whenever you want. I can take your order now or later. It's up to you."

Sean looked to Pennie questioning, "Are you hungry, Hon?"

Pennie shrugged and answered, "I'm not all that hungry yet. Maybe we eat on the way back?"

"Sounds good, so let's just get a drink for now." Sean looked up. "I think I'll try one of your Colorado brews."

The young man's face lit up. "Oh, they're terrific. The Gorge Express is brewed just for us. It's our signature brew."

"Okay, I'll try that."

Pennie put down the menu, "I'll have a Pina Colada."

The waiter made a note and then looked at White Feather pausing as if trying to figure out how to address the exotic old man.

"Frozen Margarita with salt," White Feather requested.

"Excellent. I'll be right back."

Sean leaned over to address White Feather, "So, White Feather, where are your friends?"

White Feather closed his eyes and folded his arms, "No gumption."

Sean laughed. "I must say I am surprised to see you here."

White Feather nodded. "Me too."

Sean did not quite know how to respond to that answer. "Do you know Pennie?" He waved his hand toward her.

White Feather opened his eyes. Pennie jumped in saying, "Hi, nice to finally meet you, White Feather."

White Feather forced a smile. Sean filled in with, "I've told Pennie about your help with the Ludwig triple homicide, the retirement home poisoning, and recently the double homicide at St. Jude."

They could hear the train's horns blowing at each intersection as they gradually picked up speed. Pennie smiled. "Don't you love the sound of the train's horns?"

Sean listened and agreed. Flambeau was back and heading toward the trailing cars. Sean pointed his thumb over his shoulder and asked, "What's with the paparazzi?"

White Feather stared at Sean and then smiled and nodded. "Oh, Flambeau."

White Feather shifted and then leaned back and interlaced his fingers. "Fancies himself a great photo artist."

Sean chuckled. "You know him?"

White Feather nodded again. "Just moved into St. Jude. Claims to be a famous photographer from Paris."

"Paris? I detected an accent but couldn't place it."

White Feather stated, "Not perfected, still practicing."

Sean laughed and then added, "I'm worried someone is going to get offended."

"Too late."

"I mean violently offended."

"Only matter of time."

"So, he's famous in France?"

White Feather pushed the dangling feather away from his face. "Texas. But building huge reputation here now."

Sean and Pennie laughed. Pennie commented, "He's kind of cute."

Sean inquired, "How many residents came today?"

"Just me and Flambeau."

"Well, it's not for everyone, I guess."

"Didn't invite 'em."

Sean was surprised by this answer and wondered if there might have been a schism between the Sleuthkateers. He wondered if he should ask. Then Pennie did ask, "Has there been a problem?"

"No. They can't afford train. I not pay for them."

Pennie and Sean found his candid answer humorous, but did it suggest that this man living as an indigent might have more money than he was willing to let on? Sean decided to let it pass. The waiter was bringing their drinks.

Chapter 22

Pretty Hair and Metal Boxes

Frank hated the second Tuesday of each month. It was the day that Makayla drives out to St. Jude from Rockcliffe to give free haircuts and hair styles. First of all, it just seemed wrong to have a woman cut his hair. He missed the good ole' days when you sat in a long narrow room lined on one side with customer chairs and you had your choice of reading material.

Sports Illustrated, Field and Stream, Consumer Reports, Car and Driver, and *Popular Mechanics* were some of the magazines available to enjoy while waiting. And you could listen to the barbers giving their opinions on politics, religion, and current news events. He missed the sterile white walls and checker-board floor and the smell of aftershave.

He did not miss those days when he was homeless living under a bridge and spending his days sitting in the park reading discarded newspapers and scratching his grimy, tangled, unkempt hair. So, he was thankful for St. Jude and the opportunity to take a private shower and shampoo every day and get his hair trimmed monthly. Short hair and a non-itchy scalp were blessings.

The worst part, however, was lunch. The ladies had appointments in the morning and something about a new do made the ladies feel young and beautiful and coquettish. As Frank entered the dining room, he could hear the ladies cackling and flirting in the food line with poor Walter Montgomery.

Walter looked like a big old Teddy bear surrounded by silver-haired squirrels tossing their tails, chattering and competing for the only available nut. Well, maybe Walter loved the attention, but Frank pivoted to escape.

"Frank!" Trudy shouted.

Frank froze while his mind entertained notions of bolting out the door. Before he could thaw, he felt the tender touch of Trudy's hand on his elbow. "Where are you going, handsome?"

Frank reflexively touched his hair. "I think it is time for my haircut."

"You look fine to me, sugar. Besides, it's lunch time."

Frank looked at her billowing hair around her happy round face and twinkling eyes. He didn't dislike Trudy. And he certainly wasn't afraid of Trudy. She was a happy, lively lady and he enjoyed talking to her and dancing with her on just about any other day. But, with a fresh coiffure, she was lethal!

He decided to go on offense. "Trudy, would you like to join me after dinner tonight? I think I still have some of that wonderful Chinese elixir left over from Benny's stash."

Trudy's eyes bulged and her mouth dropped open. She studied him suspiciously. "That stuff killed Benny."

Frank raised his eyebrows. "It was a miracle potion until he overdosed."

Trudy yelped and slapped his shoulder and then rushed off to chatter with her girlfriends leaving Frank free to collect his tray and drink amidst giggles and ogling eyes.

He rushed to the safety of his usual table. He found his friends sitting around the dining table deep in their individual thoughts. Ralph scooped up a mouthful of food and farted as he stuffed it into his mouth. His face reflected an epiphany. "Maybe now we can get the box back."

Albert closed his newspaper and responded, "What are you talking about, Rudolph?"

The newcomer, Cody Slade, needed clarification. "What box?"

Frank explained, "We found a mysterious metal container buried in the basement after the recent murders."

"Yes, I heard about the two bodies in the basement."

Frank continued, "We could not get the container open, so Ralph offered to blow it open. The explosion propelled the container high into the air and it came down inside the Cartel grow site."

Ralph grinned his wrinkled grin and repeated, "We can go get the box now."

Albert reminded him saying, "The authorities are still there. It is a crime scene, Rudolph."

Slade asked, "What's the significance of the box?"

Frank responded, "We think there may be a baby in it?"

Albert clarified, "The fetus from Mrs. Rommel's abortion was never found. We think it was buried in the metal box."

Slade was confused. "What's it to you?"

Ralph was indignant. "We found it. Now we want to know what's in it. What's it to you?"

Slade backed off. "Okay, it's your find. I get it."

Frank asked, "You have any contacts? Could you get us in, maybe?"

Slade shrugged. "We can walk over and see."

Red-faced and dazed, Walter set his tray down, took a deep breath, wiped sweat from his brow and asked, "See what?"

Chapter 23

Settling in on the Train

The train's deep, bellowing horns blew at each crossing in Canon City until they slipped out of town and entered the narrow canyon cut through the mountain rising to the west of the city. It was as if a tunnel had been cut through the mountain by slicing down from the top.

Sean, Pennie and White Feather enjoyed their drinks, the rapidly changing view, and the anticipation of the adventure ahead of them. Sean was beginning to relax as the realization that there was no pressure, no surprises lurking, no responsibilities today.

Today, he was just a normal person taking a ride on the train. It might even be more relaxing than one of his hunting trips. It was so rare that he and Pennie could get away and be truly away from everything.

The P.A. squawked and a man with a pleasing voice announced, "Welcome to the Royal Gorge Express. We are entering the mouth of Grape Creek and will soon be deep into the famous Royal Gorge, also known as the Grand Canyon of the Arkansas.

"That is the Arkansas River flowing beside us. The headwaters derive from the snow pack in the Sawatch and Mosquito

Mountain Ranges. From here, it then flows east into the Midwest via Kansas, and finally into the South through Oklahoma and Arkansas.

"Our journey today will take us through the gorge for about six miles. When we exit the canyon at Highway 50, we will stop momentarily at Parkdale and then reverse to come back through the canyon for a second spectacular view of the Royal Gorge and the Royal Gorge suspension bridge.

"This is one of the deepest canyons in Colorado with a maximum depth of 1,250 feet. It is also incredibly narrow averaging 50 feet wide at its base to 300 feet wide at its top as it carves a path through the granite formations of Fremont and YMCA Mountain. Now sit back, enjoy a delightful drink with our delicious cuisine and the spectacular view."

The blinding sun disappeared behind the ever rising canyon walls. Sean took a sip of his brew and scanned the people in the car. It was a natural habit to always check out his surroundings searching for potential trouble. A big man entered through the back of the car. His clothes were dusty and disheveled.

Sean recognized the fat man that was scuffling up near the terminal. He wondered where his friend might be. The scuffler joined a family mid-way in the car. They all had roughly the same hefty build and round faces. Even though they were all dressed nicely, the clothes looked rumpled and dowdy over their exaggerated figures. He assumed they all must be related.

Passengers laughed and pointed and buzzed with excitement as the train wound through the twisting canyon.

In the next car, upstairs in Vista Dome 2, the ladies of the Columbine Club applauded and cheered Florence as she finished her history of the club in honor if its 100th anniversary. Lena waved to the waitress and explained, "That's all of our program today, we'll have a more extensive business meeting next time. The waitress is going to come around for our drink orders and ... let the games begin!"

The ladies applauded again and then began chattering loudly as they started playing their card games while glancing at the walls of the gorgeous canyon passing by. Lena was happy that they had managed to adjust to the booth seating. Sometimes the strong, independent-minded ladies could fuss over the simplest changes. She glanced around to find most of them smiling and enjoying themselves.

The waitress stopped to get her drink order. "So, what game are ya'll playing?"

Lena smiled, "It's called Whist. It is an old version of bridge without the bidding."

The waitress raised her eyebrows and looked around at the happy, chattering ladies. "Noisy."

Lena snickered as the young girl took the drink orders at her table and then rushed off. When the melodic voice once again came over the P.A., they were hardly in a mood to listen. The game was the thing.

"In the early 1900s, Canon City installed a dam and pipeline in the Royal Gorge for the town's water supply. Prisoners from the Territorial Prison were used to help build the pipeline, which was mostly constructed of redwood. The system was abandoned in 1973, but remnants of it still exist today."

▉▉▉▉▉▉▉

Sean stared at the crumbling piles of wood that were once barrel-shaped. "Didn't take long for it to deteriorate, did it?"

White Feather commented, "Without water, dried wood crumbled fast."

Sean marveled at the amount of work that must have gone into the pipeline. The granite rock had to be chiseled out to provide a platform. In some places, a tunnel was chiseled through an outcropping.

Harold the Paris photographer burst through the door, spotted White Feather and joined them. "Whew! I almost was for being shot, monsieurs, madame."

Sean wanted to say, "I'm not surprised!" but reached out his hand. "I'm Sheriff Sean Bailey. This is my wife Pennie."

"I am ze Harold Flambeau." Harold jumped up to grab Pennie's hand and tried to kiss it as he finished with, "photo journalist from ze Paree." Pennie jerked her hand back and glared at the faux Frenchman.

She could tell that he had gotten a lot of mileage with the "Paris" reference, and he seemed shocked by her rejection. She chuckled and challenged him by asking, "Where is Paris, Texas?"

Harold placed his hands on his heart as if insulted. "Ah! Die lady shereef is so, how do you say, bella ..." He raised his camera but Sean instinctively grabbed it by the extended lens. "Perhaps, we could stop taking pictures for a while?"

The shocked man's eyes widened as White Feather grabbed his shirt and tugged. "Sit down, Flambeau."

The man looked perplexed and then saw someone entering the car and quickly snapped several shots. "Hey!" someone shouted. Sean looked at the man entering. It was the skinnier man involved in the scuffle. His face was red from a pummeling and his clothes were also disheveled. Curiously, he joined the bigger man. "Brothers!" Sean surmised.

"What?" Pennie asked.

"Oh! Those bruisers that were squabbling earlier must be brothers. They are sitting together now."

Harold quickly snapped several shots of the family. Sean reached for the camera, but White Feather was slightly quicker and snatched the camera, glaring at the befuddled photographer. Pennie pinched Sean on the arm. "You're off duty, remember?"

Sean glared at the shudder-bug thinking he would like to squash him like a bug. "F-a-u-x, faux, is that French?"

Harold put his finger to his chin, White Feather commented, "Close enough."

Sean smiled his most kindly smile. "So, are you a faux-tographer, Harold?"

Harold was confused, but White Feather and Pennie got it and enjoyed a good laugh. Harold squirmed in his chair, checked his camera and then rushed off. Pennie summed up everyone's thoughts when she said, "Oh, dear ...."

Conversation trailed off. Pennie's interests turned to the passing scenes outside the window. White Feather folded his arms and closed his eyes. And Sean pulled out his cell phone to check his emails. There was a message from Undersheriff Crab. It was an update on the manhunt for the cartel fugitives.

They had stolen a pickup from the Lost Trail Ranch. Sean pictured the ranch. It was only a few miles north of the grow site. The pickup was a 2008 Dodge Ram 1500 SLT with crew cab and had been spotted heading north on Highway 69. That road connected with Highway 50. If they had gone west, they would be headed for Salida. If they turned east they would be headed for Canon City.

His phone beeped as a new message from Crab appeared. "The truck was found abandoned in Veteran's Park in Canon City. From there the trail has gone cold."

Veteran's Park was next to the train depot. Sean scanned the car with renewed interest. Pennie nudged him. "What are you frowning about? You're not still worried about Harold are you?"

Sean forced a smile. "Oh, no, I didn't mean to be frowning."

White Feather spoke without bothering to open his eyes. "Harold is irritating but moves fast."

"Good point. Maybe by the time someone angers up, he's moved on."

Pennie placed her hand on his phone. "Put that away."

Sean put away his phone, but decided to stroll through the cars to look for the fugitives, just in case. "I think I'll stretch my legs and check out this place."

Chapter 24

Temporal Paradox

FRANK STARED OUT THE back door window of St. Jude at the empty bench beside the pond. This was his opportunity to safely sit on the bench without having to worry that White Feather might join him and want to resume their ongoing discussion about the dreaded time portal.

They had hashed and rehashed whether the quirky tree in front of the bench by the pond was three trees growing together or one tree repeated three times because of the disturbance caused by the time portal and he was tired of it.

Frank strolled out and plopped onto the bench happy to find that it did not shift. And happy that he could think of what ever came to mind. But, Frank could not think of anything else sitting on the bench. In fact, now he wished that White Feather was there because he had some questions to ask him.

First of all, how did White Feather know so much about his synesthesia? Had he known someone else that had this condition? And what made him think that just because he could "see" time, he also could travel back in time? And what made him presume that the bench and tree were part of a time portal?

Frank tried to imagine what White Feather would answer. To the first question, he would have to answer that he had known someone else with synesthesia. And that person would have had to have passed through a time portal because White Feather knew too much about how it worked. Now he was curious what happened to that person.

Knowing that this was a time portal must be speculation on White Feather's part because he had only been living at St. Jude for a short period of time. Perhaps there was something about it that reminded him of another place.

Albert appeared beside the bench with a newspaper folded under his arm. "May I join you, Franklin?"

"Of course."

Albert sat and laid his paper beside him. "I find it fascinating that you and White Feather spend so much time on this bench, Franklin. White Feather does not seem like a talkative sort."

"Well, no he's not. But he says a lot with few words."

"Yes. I know that to be true."

Albert studied the tree(s) in front of them. "So, this is the time portal?"

Frank was a little surprised by the mention of the time portal. Was he a mind reader? Then, he remembered that Albert had heard bits and pieces about White Feather's attempts to drag him there during an earthquake. "Yep, here it is just waiting to open up and swallow me."

Albert chuckled. "Where will it take you?"

"White Feather thinks that it is my choice."

"Interesting. Have you picked a point to return to?"

Frank was reluctant to answer. He did not want to admit he had given it so much thought. But, Albert was a great listener and he decided it would be nice to bounce some ideas off of him. "I think we all have turning points in our lives where we wonder what would have happened had we made a different choice."

"Yes. I suppose you are correct, Franklin, especially if the decision turned out badly."

"Exactly. My first marriage would be an example."

"It turned out badly for you?"

"Extremely. She was a nutcase."

Albert laughed.

"The dilemma is that if I hadn't married her, I wouldn't have had my wonderful daughter."

"That is interesting, Franklin. There have been so many books written about the consequences of changing time. No one knows the answer, really, but many fine thinkers believe that things happen regardless of what we do. That we don't really have any control over it."

"So, you think that if I go back, no matter what I do, it will turn out the same?"

"Well, frankly I don't know. I am just referring to what others have proposed. I don't know how we could know without actually going back and trying to change something."

Frank thought about it. The twists and turns of life are so complicated. "Remember the doppleganger?"

Albert laughed again. "I'm sorry about that, Franklin. We were just trying to get your mind off Elizabeth's death. You took it pretty hard."

"Oh, no, that's fine, Albert. That faked earthquake was hilarious. I deserved that. But, although I am sure that his visits to me were in a dream, he told me that if I went back not to try to hook up with ..." Frank glanced at Albert, "a certain girl from our past, that it would not turn out well."

Albert offered, "So, you believe in your subconscious that things can be changed?"

Frank tilted his head to one side. "Yes, I guess I do, don't I?"

Frank felt embarrassed. "I don't think I believe in time travel, Albert, but wouldn't that suggest that maybe I do?"

"I suppose so, but dreams are more fantasy than reality. Things happen in dreams that we know could never really happen. Besides, maybe it just reveals that you have often wondered what would have happened had you pursued that certain girl in your past."

That made Frank feel a little better. "Good point. I don't want to believe in time travel."

"I am with you on that one."

The two spent a few moments lost in thought. Then Frank stated, "It is unnerving that White Feather is so convinced that time travel is real."

Albert agreed. "Yes, that IS unnerving!"

"Do you think he has experienced it? Or, at least witnessed it?"

"That is a good question, Franklin. What do you think?"

"Maybe I'll ask him next time it comes up."

"Keep me posted."

Again the friends' thoughts drifted off. When Albert spoke again, Frank realized that their thoughts had probably traveled down the same path. "Why do you suppose White Feather decided to ride the train today?"

Frank crossed his legs. "He made the decision after he learned that Sheriff Bailey was going to take a day off and ride the train with his wife today."

"That seems odd. Why would he want to join them on a personal outing uninvited?"

"What is even more bizarre is why would he take Flambeau with him?"

Those questions became rhetorical when neither could contrive a logical explanation for either question. So they sat quietly staring at the pond until Albert upon reflection blurted out, "The temporal paradox."

Frank was lost. "Temporal paradox?"

"I finally remembered the name of that weird theory about time travel. I read about it in an article after the movie *Time Traveler's Wife* was released. They were interviewing a famous physicist, Rip or Tip or some funny name. The actor Rip Torn came to mind at the time, but I am sure that is not his name. Anyway, he disputed the idea that when one goes back in time, it is not possible to change things because then it would be possible to make the journey impossible in the first place."

"Whoa, Albert, you lost me."

"Yes, of course, I am not articulating the premise very well. Let me start at the beginning. The temporal paradox, as I understand it, states that if you go back in time to, say, kill your grandfather because he was a bad man, killing him would change your own existence and, therefore, make it impossible for you to have gone back in time in the first place because you didn't exist."

"Oookaay."

"But you could change something else if it did not alter events affecting you."

"Interesting. But here's how I look at it. When you go back, you don't go back as you are but as you were. So, if you are as you were, you would just do what you did then because you are operating with the circumstances and the brain you had then. It would never occur to you to change anything."

Albert laughed. "Excellent point, Franklin."

"It doesn't make sense to me that you could go back with your current brain without taking your body as well and then you would be a total misfit."

They both laughed. Albert declared, "The Roberts Temporal Paradox. I find it ultimately more elegant. I shall be very interested to know how White Feather counters that logic."

Chapter 25

Engine or Injun?

In the second Vista Dome car, the twenty-four ladies of the Columbine Club quickly finished off the first round of Court Whist. It was called "Coronation" and as they wrote their totals down, they ordered fresh drinks, nibbled off the snack tray and chattered while president Lena was conferring with the waitress.

"We don't want to eat until after we've played our games," Lena explained quietly.

"Are we eating now?" Asked one of the ladies. A nearby lady protested, saying, "We can't now."

"We never eat first," chimed in another.

"Lena, I thought you told them," added yet another member."

Lena raised her hands. "Calm down! We are not eating now! The waitress will only take your drink orders now." She clapped her hands and ordered them to pair up for the next round. The waitress cocked her head to one side, reached up to pinch the bulge in the wire hanging down from her ear and quietly requested assistance.

Amid the clatter of card shuffling and gossiping, the

waitresses made their way around the room as the ladies began the round called "Prosperity."

In Club Class, while Sean was strolling through the cars searching for fugitives, Pennie had struck up a conversation with a nice lady from Texas who had overheard her mention Paris, Texas. She was quite happy to boast that her husband had grown up in the little north Texas town situated across the Red River from Oklahoma and not far from the Arkansas border. "You'll have to come see the Eiffel Tower, dear."

"You have an Eiffel Tower there?" Pennie laughed.

"Ain't that where it is, honey? Complete with a big red cowboy hat!"

"You're not serious?"

"Oh, yeah, as I live and breathe, dear."

"I'll have to ask Harold about that." Pennie looked around and found that her companions had all disappeared. She glanced at the end of the car in time to see White Feather step out of the Club Class car into the Coach Class car attached next in line. He was probably going to the observation deck.

‖‖‖‖‖‖‖

The observation deck was basically a flatbed car with a railing around it. Returning from a search all the way to the end and back, Sean stepped onto the open car and noticed White Feather standing on the other side gazing at the rotting pipeline.

There were only a few people leaning against the railings

staring at the river or gazing at the passing cliffs. Sean noticed the conductor standing next to him smoking. Sean started the conversation with, "The breeze feels nice blowing off the river."

The conductor released a heavy cloud of smoke and shrugged noncommittally. It was obvious the man had escaped to the open car to get away from the passengers.

"You been with the train long?"

The man considered his question. "I been with trains for fifty years. Been with this one for two."

He flicked his cigarette butt into the river. "You a railroad fan?"

Sean shrugged. "I think they're cool, but haven't been around them very much. I grew up on a ranch. Sheriffin' now."

"Sheriff, you say? Whereabouts?"

"Wet Mountain Valley up at Rockcliffe."

"Sure, I know Rockcliffe. The old Denver and Rio Grande went up there to profit off the silver boom. It followed the Pike trail. Washed out in 1881, rebuilt in eighty-four and then was abandoned after the flood of eighty-nine."

Sean smiled. "Sounds right."

"Narrow gauge at first."

"Hmm." Clearly Sean knew very little about railroads. He reached out his hand. "Sean Bailey."

The elderly man reached out to shake the offered hand. "Chester Borden."

He avoided eye contact with the sheriff, gazing at the cliffs passing by, and then he remarked, "I worked that line as a kid."

Sean blinked and studied the face of the old man who appeared to be around 85 at most. Sean repeated the man's dates, "Eighty-nine?"

Chester looked at him quizzically and then busted out laughing. "No, not THAT line! Hell, man, how old you think I am anyway?"

Sean laughed with him. "I don't know, Chester. I guess about a hunerd and twenty or so."

Chester buckled over with laughter. "Close, my friend, close."

Sean had broken the ice. Chester warmed up and began his long, proud tale of life with the Denver and Rio Grande Railroad. While Sean listened, he glanced at White Feather again. That old Indian might just be a hundred and twenty, although it was impossible to tell.

"Want to see the engine?" Chester asked, interrupting Sean's drifting thoughts.

"Really? Sure!"

He followed Chester across the Observation car toward the Coach car. "Mind if my friend joins us?"

Chester frowned and paused. Sean pointed toward White Feather. "Want to see the engine, White Feather?"

"See me?" White Feather answered seriously.

Chester and Sean looked at each other. Sean got it, "Oh! Injun. White Feather is Native American."

The two busted out laughing again as Sean tried to smooth it over. "I meant the engine of the train."

White Feather folded his arms and remained dead serious. "I'm more interesting. Been around longer."

The two were out of control now. "You're a hoot, old timer," Chester managed to say through his laughter. White Feather good-naturedly pumped his fist and shouted, "Hoot, hoot." Then he did a little Native American-style dance.

To say the least, Sean was completely disarmed. White Feather had never shown Sean his playful side, only his somber "Native American" facade.

Pennie was surprised by her husband's rude, noisy laughter when he stepped into the Club Car with an old man in a conductor's suit holding his sides and squinting—his eyes consumed by hilarity.

"Looks like my husband has found a new friend," she said to her new friend from Texas. She felt sorry for the solemn White Feather who followed them in. Sean could get so silly and inconsiderate sometimes. She showed her pitiful face to White Feather as he walked quietly, humbly, with his arms folded and eyes closed impervious of the childlike behavior of his companions.

Sean pulled himself together long enough to check in with Pennie. "Chester is taking us up to see the engine." As if telling an inside joke, the two burst out laughing again.

"Really, Sean, are you two years old?"

As White Feather strode by, he cranked his fist and shouted, "Hoot, hoot. I'm an injun."

Pennie was shocked by this gesture so completely out of character of the traditionally stoic White Feather. However, she was not so shocked by her husband and new friend being out of control. Even onlookers were finding their hilarity contagious.

White Feather refolded his arms and followed Sean and Chester into the next car leaving passengers in Club Class with something new to buzz about.

Pennie noticed that her new friend from Texas was holding her stomach. "Oh, that old man is hilarious." She imitated him. "Hoot, hoot. I'm an injun."

Pennie was so exasperated that she was yet to see the humor in it. Her friend suggested, "Let's go see what they're serving out there."

Then Pennie laughed and said, "I'm with you."

Chapter 26

Murder!

Aꜰᴛᴇʀ ᴛʜᴇ ꜱᴇᴄᴏɴᴅ ꜱᴇᴛ, the ladies of the Columbine Club spent a moment recording their scores and rehashing the game. Maybell and Bessie announced they were in need of a bathroom break. "Where's the bathroom?"

The waitress had returned and explained, "Go downstairs and they are in the hallways."

Suddenly, a skinny black-headed man with the camera raced up the stairs and started snapping pictures. "No men allowed!" the women shouted in unison. Maybell grabbed the intruder's shirt collar and pushed him back down the stairs like she was caring a puppy by the back of his neck reading him the riot act. Bessie followed her down the stairs ready to put in her two cents.

In the Club car, Sean and White Feather returned from their adventure to "see the engine" full of energy and excitement. "So, you have to go through the back and beside the engine in a very narrow hallway. You can't imagine how noisy it is right beside the engine like that. And then you enter the control compartment where the engineer is sitting on the right in front of the controls."

Pennie tried to show interest, but it actually bored her noticeably. Sean backed off. "Well, anyway, it was pretty cool."

The waiter stopped at their table to chat. "We will be approaching the Royal Gorge Bridge shortly. We will be slowing for a few moments if you want to take pictures. Your best view is on the Observation Car if you want to head that way."

Pennie smiled brightly. "Oh! We better get out there. We don't want to miss the bridge."

The waiter added, "We will be stopping under the bridge on the way back too."

Sean addressed Pennie and White Feather, "Shall we go back to the flatcar?"

"Oh, yes."

White Feather nodded and stood.

The flatcar was already crowded with camera-ready passengers. Sean scanned the crowd but could not spot Flambeau. He was certain the man would not miss this opportunity so he assumed the faux-tographer was probably behind the crowd somewhere.

White Feather squeezed in between two people and leaned over the rail to stare at the Arkansas River rushing past in the narrow gorge. He seemed to be muttering a prayer as he held up his hands as if catching blessings falling from the sky.

A lady screamed. Bailey glanced around. Dozens on the open car were pointing toward the river and yelling, "A body!"

"It's just a log," another proclaimed.

Bailey rushed to the side of the car just in time to see what did appear to be a body release from behind a large boulder and start bobbing and flowing with the current down the river. Bailey agreed with the split crowd.

It could have been a body or it could have been a log. It was traveling too fast and the water cascading over the rocks made it impossible to see it for more than seconds at a time.

Bailey turned to White Feather. "Did you see it? What do you think it was?"

Sean waited for an answer that only came after what seemed like several minutes. "Flambeau."

"Harold? You think that was Harold?"

White Feather pointed his thumb over his shoulder. "Has pictures."

Behind him, the thin camera terrorist was snapping pictures rapid fire in all directions—pointing at the river, pointing at the canyon rim, pointing at the people on the Observation car. He was in a frenzy that appeared to have no order or purpose. There was every chance he had captured the picture of the log or body and yet every chance he had missed it entirely. Before Sean could reach him, Flambeau had pushed through the crowd and disappeared into the next car.

▐▌▐▌▐▌▐▌▐▌

Back in the Vista Dome, the ladies visited the snack tray and enjoyed a moment of gossip when the waitress announced, "We are approaching the bridge. The train will be slowing down so that you can take pictures from the open car."

"Where's that?"

"Just go downstairs and then back through the next two cars to the open Observation car."

Part of the group grabbed tables on the riverside of the car, others departed for the open car to view the incredible suspension bridge spanning the deep canyon. Once downstairs, Lena glanced down the hallway of their car to see if Maybell and Bessie might be coming out of the bathrooms.

When the hallway was empty, she decided to check on them. As she approached the bathroom door, she felt a breeze and noticed that a door at the end of the car was open. It seemed strange to her, but she ignored it. It was a nice, cool breeze.

At the bottom of the stairs to her left was a door labeled "Bathroom," She tried the door handle and was greeted with a shrill shriek! Lena jumped back and then shouted, "Maybell? Bessie?"

The tiny bathroom got quiet. Then a trembling voice asked, "Lena?"

Down the hall she heard a door open and Maybell peeked out with her pistol drawn and ready. "Did you see him?" she asked.

Lena frowned, "See who?"

"The murderer."

The door to the bathroom next to Lena opened. "The dead man?" Bessie added.

Lena looked back into the hallway. "What are you talking about? There is no one out here."

Bessie was out of breath. "Oh, it was horrible! I heard them arguing and then scuffling. They were right outside my bathroom."

"And two pops, probably a little .22 pistol."

"Then I heard the one man grunt in agony and fall against a door or wall."

"Yeah, it made a terrible racket."

Bessie pointed to the small crossway between the two cars. "Must have shot him in here and he fell out that open door and off the train."

Lena examined the floor with Maybell and Bessie hovering behind her. Sure enough they spotted a small red stain on the steps leading off the train to the outside where the river was flowing. The three gasped and Bessie shouted, "What do we do?" They heard a scream and rushed into the Club car. The passengers were rushing out the back door and through the Coach car, which led to the open car where there was a buzz in the crowd.

A half dozen members of the Columbine Club pushed onto the open car. They were like newborn puppies clumsily darting about, bumping into people searching for whatever the crowd was staring at and then sought railings to cling to. Finally, they spotted the bridge and one-by-one trained their eyes on it.

Sean looked up and spotted the shining silver thread stretching across the top of the gorge—the Royal Gorge Suspension Bridge. The fact that the bridge looked so tiny underscored the great depth of the gorge. He rejoined Pennie and White Feather and pointed up. "There's the bridge."

Pennie took out her cell phone and started snapping pictures. She asked White Feather to get one of her and Sean with the bridge in the background. The old Indian squatted down and turned the camera over and back and then back over again. "Say scalps," he jokingly said.

Columbine Club President Lena rushed out onto the car with Maybell and Bessie. When Maybell spotted the sheriff she hollered at him and pushed through the crowd to reach him. "Sheriff, Sheriff, there's been a murder!"

Bessie put on her pitiful face. "It was awful, Sean."

Lena apologized, "Ladies, please, you don't know that anything has happened."

Maybell persisted, "We saw the blood! But, the body's gone!"

Sean glanced back at the river and then tried to show concern. "Blood?"

Lena admitted, "We saw a small red stain on the steps."

Pennie hooked onto Sean's arm and whispered, "You're off duty, remember?"

Sean felt the pressure. The off-duty sheriff raised his hands. "Okay, okay, tell me what you saw exactly. Lena, you first."

"Well, okay, I found Maybell and Bessie in the two bathrooms along the hallway under our car. They overheard two men arguing and then fighting and they believe one of them got shot."

Bessie looked as if she had been caught in a fib. Maybell explained, "Well, we were in the ladies room, and we heard them arguing in the hallway. And then we heard gunshots."

Bessie blurted out, "And there's blood on the steps!"

Sean looked at Lena with concern, "Blood on the steps?"

Lena reiterated, "There IS a tiny red spot but we don't know that it is blood."

Maybell protested. "What else would it be? What are the odds it would be right where the sap got shot?"

Lena was exasperated. "We don't know anyone was shot!"

Bailey glanced at the river again. "When was this?"

Maybell glanced at her watch. "Ten minutes ago."

Lena was getting more frustrated now and stated, "There was no real evidence anything happened."

Maybell was determined to make her point. "So, why was the door open?"

"The door?"

Lena admitted, "The exit door on the river side was open at the end of the car."

Sean gave Pennie his sad puppy-dog look. "Maybe we should look at the blood stain."

Pennie rolled her eyes and shook her head. "I guess you better check it out."

Sean muttered, "Show me the stain."

As the ladies rushed toward the door, Sean glanced at White Feather. The old elder answered, "I'll find Flambeau."

Chapter 27

A Body or a Log or Tomatoes

Sean knelt down and touched the red stain on the steps. It was sticky and wet. It did not feel like blood. He raised his finger to his nose. "Smells like tomatoes."

Lena rolled her eyes. "Probably pasta."

Maybell bent over to touch the stain and smell for herself. "I don't smell tomatoes."

Sean glanced around the narrow crossway and then stood to check out the open door. He admitted to himself that theoretically a body could have been dumped into the river from the car, but it would have had to tumble ten or fifteen feet to get there.

"So where were you, ladies?"

Bessie pointed toward the end of the car. Maybell stormed over and opened the door to a tiny bathroom centered in the hallway. "I was in here about to wash up when I heard the men arguing."

"Could you tell what they were arguing about?"

Maybell answered slowly, "No, it was too muffled to understand through the door."

Bessie added, "They weren't speaking English."

Maybell added, "There was a loud crash that shook the bathroom door. Then lots of cussing ...."

"If they weren't speaking English, how could you tell they were cussing?"

"Oh, you can tell. It was just one of 'em cussing, though, the other one was whining like a baby."

Bessie joined in, "She's right. I could hear them right outside the door as they passed by. Then I heard that whooshing sound and banging as the whiney baby yelled, 'No! No!' ...."

"Two shots were fired."

Bessie added, "Then funny whispering like the air coming out of him."

Maybell waved it off. "I think it was the wind blowing from the open door."

Sean noted that Bessie was not as sure. "Anyway, it got quiet after that except for the roar of the river."

Maybell took a deep breath. "That's when I drew my gun and was going to go investigate but Lena showed up."

Bessie gave her friend a look of incredulity. Sean noticed and asked, "You remember it differently, Bessie?"

Bessie wrung her hands and muttered, "Lena didn't show up for another ten minutes."

Now Maybell was incredulous.

Lena tried to make peace. "I think Maybell did have her gun drawn when she came out."

Sean shook his head. "I hope you have a permit, Maybell. I don't want to have to haul you in."

Maybell's eyes grew large and then contemptuous. "I've been carrying this gun since I was a kid. How dare you .... What if them hoodlums would've come after us?"

Sean held up his hands. "Just saying."

Maybell straightened up and smoothed her dress in a huff. She was clearly ready for a fight. Lena touched her shoulder. "Come on, ladies, let's go look at the bridge."

Bessie and Maybell looked at the sheriff expectantly. Sean assured them, "I will look around and if I need anything, I know where to find you. Thank you, ladies."

Sean knelt down by the red stain again and examined the floor carefully. He picked up a tiny white speck and examined it closely. It was a tiny shard from a ceramic dish or cup. A tray could have been dropped and the mess not completely cleaned up.

He stood and searched the walls and ceiling for bullet holes but found nothing. He journeyed down the hallway to the galley in the center of the car. He approached the fat man who was busy over the grill. The man frowned and challenged him, saying, "Can I help you?"

"Have you been in here long?"

"Since we left the station. Who wants to know?"

Sean pulled his badge out of his pocket and the man's attitude reversed. "Oh, sorry, Sherf."

"Did anyone come by here, say about ten minutes ago?"

"People are passing by all the time. I don't pay no attention."

This person would possibly have been running."

"No. Didn't see nothing like that. But when I'm cooking over here, I can't really see the hallway very good."

Sean glanced back. The cook was right.Δ163 The hallway was partially blocked. There was a wall blocking the little hallway where the bathrooms were, so he would not have been able to see anything happening there.

"Okay, thanks. Sorry to have startled you."

The chubby man turned back to the grill. "No problem. Sorry I couldn't be no help."

Sean walked back down the hallway and stepped into the area where the exit doors were on either side. There was a smudge or stain on the open door. Blood? Maybe, maybe not. Sean backed up and pointed his finger at the door. Any slugs would have gone out toward the river. "Pow, pow."

Two shots into someone standing in front of the open door would pass outside if passing through the body. The body would fall back off the train and probably roll down the bank into the river.

Sean turned and was startled to find White Feather standing next to him. The enigma calmly informed the sheriff, "Flambeau's camera has been stolen."

Sean was concerned. "Stolen?"

White Feather turned to lead him to the scene. "Did he get a good look at the thief?"

"Young man in short pants, navy windbreaker, carrying a white canvas backpack. Wears glasses, red ball cap."

They raced through the Club car, the Coach car and out onto the Observation car. The crowds had thinned now that the bridge was no longer visible. As White Feather raced across the flatcar, Sean pulled up and grabbed his arm. "Where are we going?"

"Flambeau chased man through train."

Sean looked down the long string of cars trailing them around the bend. He really did not want to chase after weird Harold and cause more of a commotion in the rest of the train. Pennie stepped out of the next car onto the Observation car. "Pennie?"

Pennie pushed unruly hair out of her eyes. "Harold is still after him, but he has disappeared. I think he must have ducked into a bathroom."

Sean straightened and asked, "Okay, tell me what happened. Did you see the theft?"

Pennie looked at White Feather who was in no hurry to speak so she offered, "Well, Harold was taking random photos. When he stuck his camera in the face of the young man, he grabbed the camera. While Harold was trying to take it back, the man seemed to be trying to figure out how to get to the film inside. I guess that's when he realized it was digital. He took off toward the back of the train with the camera and Harold in hot pursuit."

"Why did you chase him?"

Pennie seemed to be embarrassed. "I guess I felt sorry for Harold and just got caught up in it."

Sean looked at White Feather. The old Native American shrugged, "What she said."

Sean wiped his face with his palms. "I really would like to see those pictures." Sean studied the trailing cars as he explored in his mind the futility of an extensive search. He glanced at Pennie. She had her fists on her hips and arms akimbo challenging her husband. "Don't even think about it."

Sean held up his hands. "I know, I know."

Pennie grabbed his arm and lead him back toward the Club car. "I think it is time for another drink." She looked back. "Come on, White Feather."

The old man did not budge at first, then turned away to head through the trailing cars.

Pennie smiled at Sean. "There you go, White Feather will take care of it."

Sean glanced back and chuckled. "He can probably sniff him out."

White Feather took a tumble back onto the flatcar as a young man in a navy windbreaker and red ball cap crashed onto the open car. Sean instinctively tackled the young man and they rolled to the side of the car. Somehow the agile young athlete kicked loose and dashed toward the Coach car.

Sean rolled to his feet and started to follow when he was bowled over by the skinny Harold Flambeau running at full throttle. The two tumbled across the floor of the deck and were passed by White Feather and Pennie dashing after the fugitive through the Coach car.

When they entered the lower corridor of the Vista Dome, Harold and Pennie continued at a dead run down the corridor. White Feather turned and bolted up the stairs with Sean pausing to decide, then charging up the stairs after him.

Chapter 28

Chasing the Mysterious Man

THE COLUMBINE CLUB PLAYS six variations of the game of Whist. They call it "Court Whist." The games are named Coronation, Prosperity, Conspiracy, Revolution, Confiscation and Restoration. It was during the variation "Confiscation" that the intruders appeared. In Confiscation, after the last card is dealt, there is no talking. A violator loses three points!

Lena raised a card above her head and declared, "Okay, I am laying down the last card." As she placed the card on the table, the room hushed.

Suddenly, White Feather appeared at the top of the stairs. As the wild Indian rushed down the aisle, the ladies were ready to burst, but no one was willing to break the silence. His wild hair and cowboy dress was totally offensive to the refined senses of the Ladies of Columbine who were mostly of the cowboy persuasion, but to speak would mean losing three points!

And then, just as the Indian exited the other end of the car, the unthinkable happened. A second man entered. But this time, the appearance of yet another man was just too much. Twenty-four violated women simultaneously pronounced, "You can't come in here!"

Sean stopped and scanned the protesting women, stared back at the stairs, bowed slightly, and turned to exit.

"It's the Sheriff!"

Pandemonium erupted when they recognized the sheriff. "He went that away!" Maybell shouted. Twenty-four fingers pointed in the direction White Feather had departed and confirmed, "He went that-a-way!"

"Is he the murderer?" Bessie questioned.

"Murderer!" shouted numerous others.

"There's been a murder?" others questioned.

Sean raised his hands, "There's no murderer! I'm sorry, ladies, I can't explain now. Please stay calm; you are in no danger."

Sean raced down the aisle wishing he had stated his purpose better, but he was drowned out by the loud encouragements of the excited ladies.

"You want my gun, Sheriff?" was the last thing he heard as he bounded down the front stairs back to the first floor corridor. White Feather was standing at the bottom of the stairs now looking back toward the rear of the train.

"Reversed." White Feather pronounced as he dashed down the corridor. Apparently the thief had lost Pennie and Harold. White Feather raced past the kitchen with Sean right behind him. Sean could hear the commotion and glanced over his shoulder. The Columbine Ladies were streaming down the stairs behind him led by Maybell waving her pistol.

Sean shouted, "Put that away, Maybell, or I'll have to confiscate it."

Maybell crammed it into her purse in a huff as the sheriff rushed off after White Feather. As the camera thief bounded onto the Observation car again, Sean yelled, "Stop! I'm a sheriff. You … hold it right there!"

The man glanced over his shoulder at White Feather and the sheriff with wide eyes but dashed on. Sean cursed under his breath and continued his pursuit.

Maybell was on the trail like a bloodhound leading hunters after the fox. As they would enter the front of one car, the mysterious man with Harold's camera was exiting the back end.

The P.A. announced that the train would be exiting the canyon soon and would park temporarily before starting the return trip. The train slowed causing the Columbine ladies to careen off each other like billiard balls, but they managed to stay erect and continue their quest to follow Maybell and Sheriff Bailey. Closely behind the man in the navy windbreaker the wiry White Feather led Sheriff Bailey followed by the Columbine mob yelling, "Get him … get that murdering Indian!"

The mystery man in the navy windbreaker had gained some distance on them. By the time the two men reached the end of the train, the pursued man was no longer in sight. Sean glanced out the window and determined that the train had pulled out of the canyon and was crossing Highway 50.

When they reached the last car, and rushed to the end, White Feather pointed out the window. Their man was standing in the tall weeds dusting off his clothes. "He jumped," Sean announced.

"We're not jumping, are we?" Bessie asked in a panic, but it was too late. Without hesitation White Feather leaped off the train and tucked to roll through the weeds winding up on his feet. Sean bailed out landing on his feet and then face-planted into the weeds.

Sean cursed as he pushed himself back up to his feet and dusted himself off. There had been a time when he could have negotiated the landing with grace and style like White Feather, but over the years his back had suffered from carrying his large man's six foot six inch frame. Surgeries had fused the base of his spine that had relieved his pain but left him much less flexible than in his younger days.

Sean located White Feather bounding across the hills. He took a deep breath and urged his aching body after him.

Chapter 29

Zip Line Chase

SEAN HEARD SCREAMS AND curses behind him and turned in time to see three old ladies and Pennie leaping off the train. He glanced ahead to see that White Feather and the thief were gaining distance on him. He looked back to see Pennie getting to her feet and helping up the Columbine Ladies. They appeared to be okay, so he continued racing after White Feather.

As he topped the next hill, he could see that the thief was heading for a huge wood platform. A large banner facing the highway read Canyon Zip Line Experience. A short distance behind was the familiar figure of White Feather wearing a very recognizable red flannel shirt and blue jeans. As Sean descended into the little valley, he was able to see the man with the navy windbreaker, short pants, and white backpack racing up the steps of the wood platform holding up what appeared to be a ticket. When he descended deeper into the valley, Sean lost sight of the thief.

By the time Sean reached the steps, he could barely see the red flannel shirt and blue jeans of his friend, White Feather, disappear through the pinion pines on the zip line.

He flashed his badge, "Sheriff Sean Bailey. I am in pursuit of a fugitive. Get me hooked up fast!"

The teenager stood frozen, completely at a loss for what to do. A young man maybe only a few years older but vastly more mature stepped in and strapped the sheriff to the harness and gave him a thumb up. Sean leaped off the platform only then questioning his decision.

As he flew down through the pinions, he realized that he was trapped and could not escape riding the line to the end. He tried to locate White Feather but only caught glimpses of him far in the distance. He would have to rely on White Feather to keep an eye on the perp and hope that he could keep an eye on White Feather.

Pennie and Lena made their way up to the platform first. Lena was completely out of breath so Pennie helped her to the bench to sit. "We're doing this because ...?" the practical-minded president of the Columbine Club questioned. Pennie shrugged.

Maybell and Bessie huffed and puffed their way up the steps and rushed over to the young boy strapping in the next zip liner. "We're with the sheriff!" she shouted.

"Wut?"

"We're with the sheriff. Hook us up."

"Like a deputy or somethin'?"

The more mature young man pushed the boy aside. "May I help you, ma'am?"

"Hook us up, quick, we're with the sheriff."

The man studied the determined old woman. "Hurry, he's gaining on us."

"What is this, some kinda game?"

Desperate, Maybell reached into her purse and pulled out her pistol. Bessie screamed and covered her ears. "No time to explain!" Maybell protested. The man raised his hands and backed away with eyes the size of baseballs.

Lena and Pennie rushed in. "Put up your gun, Maybell!" Lena commanded. Pennie grabbed the gun from the old woman and stuffed it into her purse. She turned to the man to explain, "There was a man on the train who stole a camera and we are chasing after him. My husband is Sheriff Bailey with the Wet Mountain Valley Sheriff's Office. I apologize for my friend, but she is very angry and very determined to catch the scoundrel."

"Yes, ma'am, but ..."

"He's a murderer!" Bessie added.

Maybell raised an eyebrow and whispered discretely, "A wild Indian."

The young man laughed but then regained control in front of the deadly serious old ladies.

Pennie corrected her. "Well, we don't know there's been a murder, but the camera may have incriminating pictures." She shrugged her shoulders and held out her hands. "Why else would he have grabbed the camera and run?"

The man shook his head. "How are ya planning on catching him now? He's gotta be two miles away by now and you're not going to be able to go any faster than he is."

Pennie put her hand on her forehead. "Oh, dear, that's right. I guess we'll have to leave it to Sean and White Feather."

The man offered, "Well, you know you could just wait over there where the line ends." He pointed to a platform down in the valley.

Pennie looked at the line heading north, then at the platform a quarter-mile away down in the valley to the east. "So, it ends up down there?"

"It's like I told the Indian. It goes down north through that valley, then back east, then south and then finishes down there."

"The Indian?"

"Yeah ... the old geezer with the funny hair." He pushed his hand above his head and wiggled his fingers to imitate the funny hairstyle of White Feather.

Maybell and Bessie exclaimed together, "The murderer!"

Pennie's eyes lit up. "That's White Feather. Is he on the zip line?"

"No ma'am. He came running after this guy with a backpack that I had just strapped in and pushed off. He wanted me to stop him, but it was too late. So, I told him what I just told you. He left to go to the end platform, I assume. Then the sheriff rushed up and demanded I strap him in and took off."

Pennie frowned and put her fists on her hips. "Why didn't you tell the sheriff what you told White Feather?"

"It was the sheriff, ma'am. He was so insistent. It never occurred to me."

Pennie shook her head. "That's Sean all right."

She turned to her friends. "Come on, ladies, let's see if we can head 'em off at the pass."

A young man in his early thirties appeared. "I got this, Danny."

"Okay, Boss."

"Come with me, ladies. I'll drive you down there in the passenger cart."

Chapter 30

Zip to Raft Pursuit

THE CANYON ZIP LINE Experience was nestled next to Highway 50 and the Arkansas River at the point where the river bends to feed through the deep canyon known as the Royal Gorge. Patrons park in a large gravel parking lot next to a gift shop and ticket office. With tickets in hand, patrons ride in modified golf carts up a series of switchbacks to reach the starting point.

It was from this point that Pennie, Lena, Maybell and Bessie had hitched a ride in one of the carts with the "Boss" back down to the parking lot and the final platform of the zip line series. About three-quarters of the way down, Maybell and Bessie spotted White Feather trudging along the asphalt path. "It's him!" Maybell shouted as she started digging in her purse.

"It's the murderer!" Bessie shouted pointing at White Feather.

"Where's my gun?" Maybell demanded.

Pennie grabbed the panicked woman's shoulder. "I put it in my purse, so you wouldn't kill somebody."

Maybell attacked Pennie's purse but Lena pulled it away and barked, "Sit down and behave!"

"But, it's the Indian ... the murderer. The sheriff has been chasing him and we have to capture the varmint."

Pennie grabbed the irate woman's shoulders. "White Feather is helping the sheriff catch the thief, Maybell. He's not a murderer; he's our friend."

Maybell continued to squirm. "I ain't takin' no chances. Gimme my gun!"

Pennie looked up to see White Feather standing calmly beside the cart. "I'll sit in the back" was his only comment. The cart continued down the path with Bessie and Maybell keeping a keen eye on the Indian.

They had only traveled a short distance when White Feather stood up in his seat and pointed at a young man with a navy windbreaker and white backpack standing on the final platform looking back up the zip line. "That's him!" he shouted.

The cart driver, the "Boss," had overheard the discussions at the starting platform and knew the significance of White Feather's announcement. He floor-boarded the gas pedal and cut across the switchbacks throwing his fragile cargo to and fro forcing old ladies to grab their hair and hang on for dear life.

The confident thief smiled and then casually strolled down the steps until he noticed the cart racing toward him with the wild Indian standing and holding onto the roll bar like George Washington standing in his boat crossing the Delaware.

The villain raced down the steps and took off running across the parking lot. Boss man swerved and bounced off the curb onto the gravel. The thief was able to race between the cars forcing the boss to have to drive down the side. Pennie shouted, "He's getting away. Go faster!"

"I'm already flooring it, ma'am."

"Who's that?" cried out Maybell.

"That's the thief," Pennie explained.

"Gimme my gun!"

By the time they reached the end of the parking lot and turned to head for the exit, the thief had raced out of the parking lot, over train tracks and disappeared down the entrance road. As the cart reached the tracks, horns honked and brakes squealed as the cart riders braced for impact from what they first thought was the train bearing down on them.

They safely bounced across the tracks to the top of the road and could see that traffic was in chaos where the thief had crossed Highway 50. He was now diving onto a passing raft on the Arkansas River.

After briefly scuffling with the raft guide and knocking him into the river, the thief barked commands and the rafters obediently began digging their oars into the water.

"We're gonna lose him!" Maybell screamed as she pulled her pistol out of Pennie's purse and fired two shots at the raft.

"No!" shouted Pennie, "you'll hit one of the rafters."

"I ain't aimin' at rafters."

White Feather reached down and extracted the gun from the wild woman."

"Gimme my gun back, Injun! You're next," Maybell protested as she pounded on his knee.

"You hit the raft!" Boss proclaimed. Sure enough the raft was deflating rapidly. The thief commandeered the next raft passing by while another group pulled up to rescue the rafters in the deflating raft. Boss slammed on the brakes as the cart skidded up to the stop sign at Highway 50. "What should I do?"

White Feather pointed the gun past his head. "Cross to the bridge."

Boss glanced left and floored it again. Horns honked and cars skidded, but they managed to get across Highway 50 without getting hit or causing a serious accident. Boss stopped the cart on the bridge over the river. White Feather was off the cart and over the edge before anyone could blink. Maybell was right behind him.

The others bailed out of the cart in time to see White Feather and Maybell being hauled out of the river by people in another raft. They could see White Feather start commanding the rafters to chase the thief's raft. In only a matter of seconds they disappeared into the deep Royal Gorge Canyon.

Pennie was the first to speak. "We need to go find Sean."

They heard a scream. They watched Bessie descending into the river holding her nose. Ker splash. Pennie leaped in after her. Fortunately, it was a busy day for rafters and they were quickly rescued.

"What do we do?" Boss pleaded.

Lena turned back to the cart. "Let's go find the sheriff."

The water got rough quickly after entering the gorge. White Feather was straining to keep sight of the thief. Maybell was having trouble clutching the slippery raft as it pitched and bucked in the billowing rapids. No one was rowing. Everyone was just hanging on until White Feather commanded, "Must row. Thief getting away."

The raft guide took over and whipped the team of rookies into gear. To Maybell, it felt like they were going one hundred miles-per-hour through the gorge. Behind them in another raft, Pennie hugged Bessie and asked, "Are you okay?"

The drenched woman spit water out of her mouth and proclaimed, "Hot, damn."

Pennie doubled over laughing as did the other rafters. The guide shouted, "Pull into shore." He pointed at a spot on the left and encouraged his group to row hard.

Pennie and the guide helped the shivering Bessie out of the raft and safely to shore. Pennie thanked the guide. "We'll be fine. I'm calling 9-1-1."

As if on cue, Boss drove up in the cart with Sean and Lena on the railway tracks. "You guys okay?" Sean questioned as he leaped out of the cart and helped Pennie and Bessie up the steep bank and into the cart.

"No cell phone coverage!" Pennie alerted Sean.

The Royal Gorge Express horns blew loudly as the train came around the bend. Sean stepped in front of the cart and began waving his arms to try to attract the attention of the engineer. The horns blew again as the boss pulled the ladies out of the cart and off the tracks. Sean stopped waving and held his hands high as the huge locomotive drew closer and closer. Sparks flew from the squealing wheels. At the last minute, he jumped to the side as the engine nudged the passenger cart several yards down the tracks before stopping.

Engineer Kesler stuck his head out the window and shouted, "What are you fools doin' on the tracks? You damned near got killed!"

Sean was dusting off his pants and yelled up, "It's me, Lee, Sheriff Bailey."

"Sean? What in blazes is goin' on?"

"We're trying to chase down a fugitive, Lee. He has commandeered a raft and is heading down the river."

"And you expected to catch him in that thing?"

Sean shook his head. "This fine gentleman was trying to rescue those poor ladies, Lee. No time to think, you know?"

"Can you move that cart?"

Boss quickly got into the cart. The wheels spun and the cart moved ahead a few yards before he stopped and threw up his hands. The wheels would not cross the tracks.

A door in the nose of the engine flew open and Lee hopped off the steps onto the tracks. Conductor Chester Borden came running up alongside the engine. "What's goin' on, Lee?"

"Sheriff was on the tracks in this cart rescuing damsels in distress and chasin' a fugitive."

Chester shook his head. "What were you thinking?"

"It was foolish, I know guys, but let's get this cart off the tracks and the ladies back on the train so we can get going."

They rushed over to the cart and lifted the front end over while Chester grumbled, "You ain't gonna catch no raft now, friends."

Chapter 31

The Body

Ｔ HE GUIDE HAD PRODUCED vests for his new guests. Maybell had been moved to the center of the raft where she assumed the role of cheerleader. White Feather had grabbed an oar and was rowing hard with the others since the raft with the thief appeared to be getting farther away.

"Row harder! He's getting away!" Maybell commanded.

Either their forceful rowing was working or the thief's raft was now slowing. Then White Feather realized that a mutiny appeared to be taking place on that raft.

Maybell also noticed. "They're fightin'. Get him! Sock him! That's it!"

In the scuffle, the man in the navy windbreaker was shoved overboard. White Feather pointed and motioned at his raft guide. The guide nodded and started maneuvering the raft toward the flailing lost cargo. And the raft the thief had been in appeared to be desperately trying to slow down to rescue him as well. The man was fighting to swim to shore when he collided with a boulder and went limp.

"Ouch!" Maybell screamed, "Oh, dear, is he dead?"

The stream carried him swiftly on downstream past the raft he had fallen out of and on beyond until he disappeared.

White Feather slumped down dejected. Then he heard the horns of the Royal Gorge Express. "Take us to shore!" he commanded.

The rafters managed to hail the train to a stop and White Feather and Maybell were met by Sean and train staff and helped onto the train. Lena led Maybell away stating firmly, "We need to get you and Bessie into dry clothes. The conductor has provided some nice coveralls for you both."

White Feather shook his head. "Thief hit a rock."

Sean rubbed his forehead. "He dead?"

White Feather shrugged. "Probably."

Sean checked his phone and determined he had two bars. He called Canyon City Search and Rescue to explain the situation. They reported that they would search the river for the body.

White Feather put things into perspective. "No camera, no pictures."

Sean gazed out the window. "You're right. We need those pictures."

⫴⫴⫴⫴

Sean and Pennie sat quietly staring out the window at the passing canyon. White Feather appeared to be asleep and Harold was sitting quietly staring at nothing. Sean and Pennie were no longer in a mood to relax and enjoy the train even though now things had calmed down. The train began to slow. "Must be coming up to the Royal Gorge Bridge," Sean remarked.

White Feather opened his eyes and looked around. He frowned and then closed his eyes again. Harold was sitting quietly like a little boy who had lost his Teddy bear.

"Want to go out on the deck?" Sean asked Pennie.

Pennie shrugged and pushed her chair back. From the front door of the car, Florence and Elizabeth rushed in and made a beeline for the sheriff, but they stopped short when they saw White Feather.

In whispers they cornered the Sheriff. "You caught him!" They pointed at White Feather.

"No, no. White Feather is a friend. He is sitting with us," Sean whispered back.

"But, you were chasing him earlier. We saw you when he ran through our car," Florence said.

Sean chuckled. "We were both chasing that thief. It just looked like I was chasing him."

They raised their eyebrows as if filled with doubt. Florence declared, "Well, Maybell said he killed a man and threw him off the train."

"And we've talked to people who saw the body floating down the river," added Elizabeth.

Pennie was getting impatient. "I saw it too. It was just a log."

"Pssst." Florence and Elizabeth drew back as if insulted. Sean touched Elizabeth's shoulder. "I saw it too. If it was a body, it will turn up."

Elizabeth smiled but Florence continued to glare at Pennie. Pennie seemed unconcerned as she turned to head for the Observation car.

As they stepped out on the open deck, Sean's phone buzzed. It was the Canyon City Search and Rescue (CCSAR). "Sean Bailey," he answered.

"We've spotted the body, Sheriff, at the base of the bridge. We need you to check it out for us and help get a halter around it."

"Roger, copy that. I think we are approaching the bridge now."

He looked up but could not see the bridge. A helicopter appeared from behind the wall ahead. CCSAR replied, "We see the train approaching. Can you get with the engineer and pull on up to the platform where the old tram used to take people down?"

"Used to?"

"Yeah, it was destroyed by the fire. We are dropping a team at the base of the old tramway."

"Roger, out."

He hung up the phone and gave Pennie his whooped tiger look. She waved him away. Sean searched his contacts for the engineer's phone number he had collected earlier. "Hi, Lee. Just talked to Search and Rescue and they have located a body where the tram used to come down to the river. They want us to assist extraction. Can you pull close?"

The engineer responded, "We are approaching there now. Want to come up?"

"Sure."

Pennie squeezed his arm and pointed up. The Search and Rescue helicopter was hovering near the bridge now visible spanning the canyon rims. Sean smiled, "Want to see the engine?"

Pennie smiled and pumped her fist. "Hoot, hoot."

White Feather stood and pumped his fist. "Hoot, hoot."

‖‖‖‖‖‖‖‖

"Hi, Lee, this is my wife, Pennie. And you know White Feather."

Lee Kesler was an average-sized man wearing baggy coveralls. He had a great Irish face with a grand smile, surrounded by a white mustache and beard. "Welcome, Pennie."

His voice boomed over the loud engines behind them as he shook her hand. "There's the body up there by the concrete platform. Looks like it got caught in the whirlpool."

Sean spotted the body jammed against the platform. He dialed CCSAR. "We've got eyes on the body. I am departing the train to get a closer look. It is quite a reach to get down to it from the platform."

"Roger."

Lee set the train brake and pointed up the arroyo. "They're lowering someone now."

Then he descended the steps centered in the control room leading into the nose of the engine. He opened a door in the nose of the train and jumped down to the tracks. He waited for Sean to join him.

Sean gave him a thumb up as he descended the engine to the tracks. Lee cautioned, "Be careful, Sheriff, the tracks are suspended here ... no shoulders."

Sean noticed the huge braces spanning the river mounted in the wall on the other side. They angled down to the tracks and the walls on this side.

Lee explained, "Those braces used to hold up the bridge for the train. But, trains today are too heavy so they built a concrete foundation underneath grounded in the base of the canyon underwater to support the bridge.

From there Sean was able to step on the crossties and work his way across the short modified suspension bridge. As he approached the platform, he got a good look at the water-logged body of the poor camera thief bobbing up and down and bumping against the concrete platform.

By the time the sheriff had crawled over the railing onto the platform, the search and rescue team joined him. "Hi, Sean. What have we got?"

Sean nodded to the four men recognizing the Canon City coroner. "The body is temporarily trapped over here against the platform in a whirlpool." The men checked out the situation and then got to work. Sean was impressed by their professionalism. They hardly had to talk to each other. The lead, Gary, contacted the helicopter pilot saying, "John, we're not going to be able to carry him out."

"Roger that."

"We'll load him on the train."

Gary glanced back at the conductor standing on the tracks now. He waved and reported in on his radio.

Within minutes they pitched the backpack over the rail. Sean unzipped the pack and was surprised to find the backpack filled with not only Harold's camera but purses and billfolds. The man was more than a camera thief.

Sean helped lift the body over the rail onto the platform. The body was checked medically and the coroner declared him deceased. Sean pulled the man's own wallet out of his pants pocket. Then out of the corner of his eye, Sean saw something move. It was White Feather kneeling beside the backpack and pulling down the back of his own jacket.

"What are you doing?"

"Check your wallet?"

Sean slapped his hip. "Got it."

White Feather stood. "Me too."

Sean studied his old friend for a moment before concluding why he'd been so persistent in chasing the thief. "You weren't interested in the camera. You were after your own wallet!"

Chapter 32

Pictures

AS THE TRAIN PULLED away from the platform and modified suspension bridge, Sean and White Feather rejoined Pennie and Flambeau. Pennie confessed, "I took the liberty of ordering our meals. Harold and I are starving."

As if waiting for her announcement, the waiter came hustling down the aisle with a tray full of food. She was anxious to see if White Feather would be pleased. He did not hesitate to begin eating, nor did Sean. She relaxed. She had got it right.

The Vista Dome was alive with chatter and the clicking sounds of cards being shuffled, dealt or played. Lena had kept reminding them to play fast so they could complete all the games and have a late lunch. Maybell looked across the table at her friend, Bessie, and whispered, "I still think the Injun did it."

Bessie said a little too loudly, "Apparently there was no murder."

Maybell replied in a huff, "Bull pucky. You were there; you heard it!"

Maybell's card partner, sitting next to Bessie, gasped. "You saw a murder?"

Bessie explained, "We didn't SEE anything. We heard something when we were in the bathroom."

Bessie's card partner was intrigued. "You heard a murder?"

Bessie grabbed her arm. "Shhh! We heard two men arguing and what sounded like two gunshots."

Maybell clarified, "Small .22 caliber we think."

"You should tell the sheriff."

"We did. He thinks we were just hearing things."

"What are you going to do?"

Maybell patted her purse and winked. "I'm keeping an eye on that Injun."

Now Maybell's partner remembered. "Didn't the sheriff chase an Indian through here earlier?"

Maybell got excited. "That was him! That's the murderer."

Back in the Club car, a server appeared and asked, "Are you Sheriff Bailey?"

"Yes."

She handed him a folded note. Sean read it.

Pennie was concerned. "What's it say?"

Sean looked up at White Feather and said, "It's from Doug at SARCC. His note reads: 'The body of a cartel fugitive has washed ashore at Veteran's Park. The third fugitive may be on the train.'"

Pennie looked away. "Crap."

Sean pulled out Flambeau's water-soaked camera and asked, "How long do you think it will be before we can check the pictures, Harold?"

Flambeau waved his hands back and forth, "No, no. No pictures, mon ami."

"They're ruined?"

Flambeau reached into his pocket and produced an SD card. "Ze card in camera is empty. New card put in before stolen, you see."

Sean's eyes bulged slightly. White Feather opened his eyes and smiled. Pennie beamed and reached into her purse to pull out her notebook. "Plug it in here. We can look at the pictures!"

As they began clicking through the pictures, it was clear that Flambeau was thorough, but also clear he was no great photographer. People were shot from all angles, sometimes chopping off their heads or shot so close the faces were unrecognizable. The collage prompted quiet chuckles from everyone except for the proud Flambeau. Sean could not restrain himself. "Well, you are definitely thorough, Harold."

"Wee, of course, as per instruction from Wit Fetter."

"Who?"

"Me." White Feather indicated by bumping his thumb against his chest.

Sean frowned and studied his omniscient friend. "How did you know we would need pictures today?"

"Hunch."

"Oh, no, you're not getting away with that this time. It was more than a hunch and you know it."

"Evidential deduction."

Pennie giggled. Sean shook his head. "What evidence?"

"Fugitives headed north."

"Okay, but they could have gone to Salida or anywhere. What made you think they would take the train?"

"You."

"Me?"

"Fate."

Pennie got it. "Of course, fate wouldn't let you take a day off."

White Feather pointed at a face on the screen of a big man in khakis standing in the background with black shaggy hair and a dark complexion."

"That's him!" Sean exclaimed. "That's the cartel boss."

"Oh, dear!" Pennie gasped as she searched the faces in the Club car.

Sean continued paging through the pictures stopping at a set of pictures taken of a corridor and stairs. Two men were standing in the corridor. One was the cartel boss in khakis, the other a short, stocky man in camouflage. "Good work, Harold. You've placed them in the Vista Dome corridor!"

Pennie asked, "Why is that important?"

"It confirms Maybell's and Bessie's story that they heard two men arguing and possible gunshots."

Sean skipped through pictures of the Columbine Ladies in an uproar, people dining peacefully, people dining in an uproar, crowds on the Observation car looking up pointing or taking pictures of the bridge. He stopped at pictures of the river. He placed his fingers on a spot and expanded it. "Definitely a body ... not a log."

White Feather pointed to the time stamp on the picture. Sean made a note.

Now Sean scanned more quickly through pictures of people in the other cars, more pictures on the Observation car, and finally pictures of the thief picking pockets and then the floor right before the SD card was being traded out.

Sean looked up and summarized. "Harold you have done a masterful job of documenting this trip including the fugitives AND the pickpocket. So, we know the cartel boss was on the train. The question is whether he still is or jumped off at some point. Shall we start searching?"

Pennie grabbed his arm. "I don't know, Sean, he is a murderer. He has a gun and you don't have your gun with you. We are defenseless. Besides, when the train stopped and reversed, he must have figured out it wasn't going anywhere. Why would he stay on?"

Sean rolled his head. "Those are all good points, Pennie, but isn't it our duty and responsibility to make sure the passengers are safe?"

"Not today."

White Feather pushed into the aisle and stood up. "I can be discreet."

Pennie laughed. "Oh, sure, no one will notice you."

White Feather ignored her and headed toward the back of the train.

Sean held out his hands. "At least let me check the Vista Domes. Like you say, he's probably jumped off the train by now anyway."

Pennie huffed and waved him off.

Chapter 33

The Search

T HE OLD MEN, EXCEPT for Slade, were gasping for breath after the long walk up and over Cemetery Hill. They approached the arroyo in back of the grow site and decided to rest before crossing.

The metal building along the backside of the compound blocked most of their view of the site, but they could see guards on the north side of the fence. Slade pointed and shared, "I know Melton over there, but he is a stickler. Not likely gonna let us enter a crime scene especially with CBI around.

With renewed energy the old men plodded across the arroyo and approached Deputy Melton. Melton looked the sweaty old men up and down. He addressed Slade, "Got something to report, Cody?"

Slade answered, "Nothing stirring at St. Jude."

Melton countered, "I wouldn't think so. One fugitive was shot over at Lost Trail Ranch. One was shot on the Royal Gorge Express and the body washed up at Veteran's Park. The other is still on the train or in the gorge somewhere."

Slade shrugged. "My job is done sounds like."

The Sleuthkateers glared at Slade in shock. Slade glanced at them and then questioned Melton, "The boys have a metal container they want to retrieve from the site."

"What's it doing over here?"

He chuckled. "They were trying to blow it open and launched it over the fence."

Melton looked at Ralph and laughed and then explained, "All the contents have been transferred to the warehouse in Pueblo. You'll have to wait until after the investigation to claim it."

Ralph farted.

ⅢⅢⅢⅢ

Sean felt naked without his service pistol. He decided to check the Columbine party in Vista Dome 2. Remembering their "no men" rule, he paused at the top of the stairs and waved at Lena. After a short wait, Lena noticed him and left her game to walk over.

"I'm sorry to bother you, but I need to search your area."

"What for?"

"It's urgent, Lena. I won't take long."

Lena turned and shouted,"Ladies ... ladies ... listen up! Sheriff Bailey wants to search this area."

Lots of agitated voices demanded, "What for?"

"I don't know. It's official business," Lena responded.

She invited him to pass her and whispered, "Good luck!"

"Thanks."

Sean stepped in and held up his hands. "I'm sorry to disturb you. This will only take a minute."

Maybell shouted, "You finally looking for the murderer?"

Another lady spoke up and said, "I thought you caught him."

Maybell countered saying, "That was a petty thief."

Several asked, "There's a murderer?"

Sean waved his hands in the air. "Ladies, please, there's nothing to be concerned about. I just need to walk through and check for evidence regarding the pickpocket. Have any of you lost anything?"

The ladies gasped and started digging through their purses. Sean took this opportunity to walk through the car. One lady stopped him. "My glasses are missing!"

Her friend pointed at her head. "You're wearing them, silly."

In the center of the car, two young waitresses were huddled in a small booth. Sean approached them. "Hi, I'm Sheriff Bailey from Rockcliffe. Can you communicate with the rest of the staff from this Dome car?"

"Yes," they replied in unison.

"Can you tell them to be on the lookout for an Hispanic male about five foot ten wearing khaki pants and shirt?"

Their eyes got wide as they glanced at each other and one asked, "Can we do that?"

"Better ask Chester," said the other girl.

"Okay, I'm going to ask the conductor. Hold on."

Sean wanted to slap his forehead like a dummy. "Of course, that's even better. Ask him to meet me in the first Club car."

The waitress nodded in reply and pinched the bulge on the cord hanging down and gave the message to the conductor.

Sean quickly checked the front of the car where everything appeared in order. He turned to walk back down the aisle. "Everyone have everything?"

Maybell waved her pistol. "Don't worry, Sheriff, if that murderin' Injun comes up here, he'll wish he'd stayed off the train while he had a chance."

Sean shook his head like a disappointed father. "Maybell, what'd I tell you about keeping that gun in your purse?"

Frustrated, Maybell stuffed the gun back into her purse. Sean walked over to her. "That Injun you are referring to is working with me on the case. I can assure you he is not a murderer."

"Oh, yeah, well who IS the murderer then?"

"No one has said anything about a murder, Maybell."

"Hogwash. Me and Bessie said something about a murder. We heard it."

Sean felt himself getting tense. He could not dispute her and be honest. But, he could see that she was stirring up the ladies. He had to come up with something. "Okay, okay, I'll let you in on a little secret, but you have to keep it to yourselves."

He paused to give each lady a stern look. "It is possible that the pickpocket had an accomplice. We are looking for a person of interest. He's about five foot ten inches tall, unruly black hair and dark complexion."

Maybell pulled out her pistol again and shouted, "It's the Injun. I told you he was suspicious."

Sean gulped and shook his head. "Maybell, give me that pistol! I have warned you enough times."

Maybell pointed the pistol at Sean. "Nobody's taking my pistol as long as that murderin' Injun is on board!"

Bessie snatched the gun out of Maybell's hand and passed it to the sheriff. "Really, Maybell, you need to get a handle on it, girl. The Sheriff here will keep us all safe."

Sean took the pistol and stuffed it into his pocket. "Thanks, Bessie. Maybell, you'll get it back when we return to the terminal. For now, try to stay calm."

"But, I need my gun. What if that murderin' Injun shows up?"

"No. It's not the Injun! The Injun's name is White Feather, by the way. Our suspect is bulky, like me, and is probably Cuban."

Florence gasped and reported, "I saw him! He was wearing dirty khakis and has a mustache. Oh my gosh, is he dangerous?!"

"Where did you see him, Florence?"

"Oh, dear, let me think. Oh! He was on the open air car when that man's camera was snatched."

"Okay, that was him. Have any of you seen him since then?"

The ladies glanced around at each other and started a buzz. Sean held up his arms again. "Okay, okay, if you see him, don't approach him. Just let me know and let me handle it." He looked directly at Maybell.

"Gimme my gun and I'll take care of him."

"When we get back to the terminal, not before." Sean stomped out.

He walked through the infamous corridor where Maybell and Bessie claimed they had heard men arguing. Technically, this should be a crime scene, he thought. He checked the bathrooms, storage rooms, and then passed by the center kitchen area where staff appeared to be taking a break. He checked the bathrooms and storage down that narrow corridor before stepping across to Vista Dome 1.

The Vista Dome 1 corridor was vacant and quiet. He checked the bathrooms, storage rooms, kitchen on that floor and then went upstairs. The tables were full and the passengers were quietly talking, eating and drinking. They paid little attention to him as he strolled through and checked the bar in the center.

Pennie was probably right. The Cuban would have had plenty of opportunity to jump off the train. And if he was smart, he would have. Sean decided to return to the Club car to wait for the conductor and White Feather's report.

Chapter 34

Eyebrows and a Conductor

FRANK SAT STIFFLY IN the barber chair under the smock with his arms snug against his sides and his hands clasped tightly in his lap hoping not to accidentally touch the stylist when she leaned in. "What have you been up to, Mr. Roberts?"

Frank's voice was weak and raspy. "Not much."

Makayla talked softly and worked efficiently at cutting his hair. "I hear you moved into a new room."

Frank gasped. "Who told you that?"

"Oh, I don't know. One of the ladies mentioned it, I think."

Frank huffed. Makayla continued to comb and snip as Frank watched her in the wall mounted mirror. Makayla was young, attractive and serious. Frank had learned that she was a cowgirl with a horse and interests in western fashion and ranching life. She was quite thin but looked athletic in a rugged sort of way. He felt embarrassed by his snippy remarks. He decided to try again. He took a deep breath and made an effort to relax. "It's a really nice room with a great view of the Sangres."

He could see in the mirror that her thoughts had drifted away. She paused and glanced at him in the mirror, forced a smile and answered, "Oh? That's nice."

As she resumed her work, Frank sensed that Makayla probably had no serious interest in his room or his life. Why would she? He sensed that she was a kind person but that behind those dark sad eyes that were carefully analyzing the length of the hair she had swooped up with her comb, there was a complicated story, possibly a sad story. He sensed that her deepest thoughts might be about planning her weekend, or maybe reliving a recent date, or agonizing over a troublesome relationship.

He let his thoughts turn to his own sad, pathetic story. Was he lucky to be old and have no complicated life or relationship to perplex his thoughts? His mind jumped to his last snippy remarks to poor Trudy. How sad Trudy's life must be. She had built her life around her late husband. Now he was gone. The money was gone.

She was stuck in an institution surrounded by old desperate men and women living out their last days with no future, no real hope, just comfort and security to cling to at St. Jude. Why had he treated her so cruelly? Was he afraid of her? Was he afraid of commitment at his age?

He actually admired Trudy's irrepressible optimism and innocent delightful personality. She deserved better. She and the other ladies deserved to feel beautiful and young and coquettish once in a while. Who was he to step on that small moment? They, like him, need to be needed, appreciated and loved. Maybe he should take Trudy more seriously. It might be good for both of them to establish a closer relationship.

"Want your eyebrows trimmed?" Makayla startled him. He had never thought about trimming his eyebrows. No barber ever asked him that. Maybe that was a girl thing. Of course, Makayla was a hair stylist and not a barber. He shrugged, "If they need it, I guess."

||||||||||

Sean rejoined Pennie and Flambeau. They had ordered drinks and were silently staring out the window. Pennie seemed disinterested but still asked, "Find anything?"

"No. It's clear up front."

"The engine clear?"

"No. Maybell is convinced that White Feather is a murderer and plans to shoot him when she sees him. I had to redirect their attention, so I told them that the Cuban boss might be the pickpocket's accomplice."

Pennie was grinning in a way that told him he had missed something. "What?"

"That's all very interesting, Dear, but I was asking about the train engine, not our Injun friend."

"Oh!" Sean realized that he had not checked the train engine. "He wouldn't go there. Surely the door is kept locked ...."

Pennie rolled her head and then sipped her drink. Flambeau began to snore. The more Sean thought about it, the more it bothered him. The waiter appeared. "Can I get you anything?"

"I'll have a coffee, black, please."

The waiter wrote it down and started to leave when Sean asked, "Does the engineer keep the door locked to the engine?"

The waiter looked puzzled. "I don't know if it is locked. He's pretty friendly though. You might try knocking."

It was not the answer Sean wanted to hear. What if the Cuban knocked on the door?

Chester appeared and sat down next to Sean. "The waitress, Acacia, said you wanted to see me?"

Sean glanced around to make sure no one was listening. "We may have a fugitive on the train. He's Cuban, about five foot ten, mustache, wearing dirty khakis."

"Fugitive from what?"

"We raided a number of illegal grow sites Tuesday and he and two others escaped. Now he has apparently murdered his two accomplices and may be on this train."

Chester thought about it and then shook his head. "Why would he be on this train? We don't go anywhere."

"I don't think he knew that."

"Well that has to be a surprise for him, I'll bet," Chester commented.

"I think it made him furious and he blamed his friend. They got into an argument and he shot him."

"On the train?" Chester asked.

"Just a theory. I don't have any proof at this point." Sean shrugged.

"What do you want me to do?"

"Keep an eye out for him. Notify the staff to watch for him too."

Chester said, "I can do that. But he's armed and dangerous. Should we evacuate the train?"

"My guess is he has already jumped off the train by now."

"That would make sense. All right, I'll notify the staff and let you know if we spot him."

White Feather walked up and nodded at the conductor. Sean asked, "Find him?"

White Feather shook his head. "Not back there." He pointed his thumb over his shoulder as he folded his arms and closed his eyes.

Chester was speaking into his radio notifying staff. When he finished, Sean asked, "Did you notify the engineer?"

Chester returned to his radio. "Lee? Lee, pick up."

Chester looked panicked. Sean patted Maybell's gun in his pocket as he looked at Pennie. "We better go check."

Pennie was concerned. "You're unarmed, Sean!"

Both White Feather and Sean instantly produced handguns. They looked at each other and laughed. Penny was livid. "You told me you left your gun in the truck!"

"I did, Sweetheart. This is Maybell's pistol. She wouldn't stop flashing it around so I had to confiscate it."

Pennie backed off slightly. "Is it loaded?"

Sean checked. "Yes, two bullets missing."

Pennie remembered. "The slugs are in a raft somewhere."

Chapter 35

The Capture

As Sean, Chester and White Feather were about to exit Vista Dome 1, they felt the train slowing. They looked outside to see that the train was stopping. Chester guessed, "He's reversing direction. Gonna make a run for it!"

They rushed through the boxy power car, down the narrow hallway beside the noisy engine and then stopped at the back door to the engine compartment. Sean and White Feather took opposite sides of the engine door with drawn pistols. Sean nodded to Chester to get behind him. He checked the door. It was not locked. He nodded at White Feather, pushed the door open partially and yelled, "Lee! It's the sheriff."

Sean barely glimpsed the Cuban before he dove for the door and slammed it shut. He heard a latching sound and found the door to be locked. He started banging on the door and shouting, "Sheriff! Open up!"

They felt the train lurch and the engines getting louder. Sean started pounding harder. The engines were getting louder still. They could feel the train picking up speed. Sean turned to Chester. "You have a key?"

Chester pulled out a ring of keys and searched for the engine compartment key. Sean asked, "Is there any way to stop the train from outside the engine control room?"

Chester smiled broadly and declared proudly, "Sure is!"

"How?"

"There's an emergency pull at the end of the Vista Dome 1. Puts the train into emergency mode. Puts on the brakes."

"Gimme the key to this door and you go shut us down."

Chester rushed off. White Feather held up his gun and nodded. Sean inserted the key and waited. After several minutes the engines shut down and the brakes applied forcing Sean and White Feather against the wall opposite the control compartment. They could hear shouting inside the control room.

Sean unbolted the door, nodded to White Feather and then threw open the door. The engineer was lying on the floor with a head wound. The door in the center of the nose of the locomotive was open and they saw the Cuban jump to the ground and start running down the tracks. Sean shouted out the door, "Stop! Stop or I'll shoot!"

The Cuban reached back and fired several shots at the train and then disappeared around a bend in the tracks. Sean scrambled out the door and jumped to the tracks and raced off after the fugitive.

When he got to the bend he could see that the fugitive had a lengthy head start. He shouted at him but was sure he could not be heard above the roar of the Arkansas River right next to the trackbed. Sean took a deep breath and raced on. The steep granite walls of the gorge meant that the fugitive was trapped and would have to stay on the tracks unless he leaped into the raging river.

Suddenly the deafening horns of the train blasted from behind. Sean almost leaped into the river himself. He looked back to see Chester, Lee and White Feather grinning at him through the windows of the locomotive that was inching toward him. The train stopped and Sean climbed back up into the cockpit. The wounded engineer smiled proudly and restarted the train. Sean was grateful he would no longer have to chase after the man.

Quickly the train caught up to the Cuban who desperately resorted to climbing up the steep, slippery wall of the canyon. As the train got closer, Lee blasted the horns. The startled Cuban lost his grip and tumbled down onto the tracks. Lee threw on the brakes and they hung on as the Cuban disappeared in front of the train. Sean raced down the stairs of the engine nose and threw open the door. The Cuban lay across the tracks mere inches from the train cringing. Sean leaped out the front door onto the tracks and stood over the Cuban.

White Feather followed Sean out onto the tracks and handed him a necklace with colorful beads on a leather strap. Sean accepted the necklace and looked at the Indian curiously. "Am I supposed to bless him?"

White Feather snatched the necklace back, untied the leather strap and let the beads cascade off of it. He knelt down and tied the Cuban's wrists behind his back with the leather strap.

Lee and Chester had a good laugh. White Feather pulled his pistol and held it on the Cuban while Sean secured his pistol in his pocket and lifted the prisoner to his feet while informing him of his rights. The Cuban repeated, "No hablo Engles ..." over and over.

Chapter 36

Lost Their Marbles

Albert lowered the newspaper enough to peek over the top edge to see his four friends sitting uncomfortably around a rickety old card table. Frank drew a card from the draw pile and added it to the five cards in his hand.

"Where'd you get this game, Ralph?"

Ralph reached into a bowl teetering in his lap, pinched three kernels of popcorn and stuffed them in his mouth before answering, "Slade."

Frank checked his cheat sheet, discarded a Joker, then took a marble from his starting box and replaced his partner Monty's marble to set it in front of Monty's home spot. Slade answered passively, "Texas."

"Texas?"

Ralph wiped butter from his fingers on his blue Hawaiian shorts and drew a card. Slade expanded saying, "Little town near Amarillo."

Ralph played a seven and moved his marble seven spaces and grabbed his beer to gulp down a couple of swallows. Slade frowned. "You know you can split that don't you?"

Ralph scanned his cheat sheet. "Crap." He burped loudly, set down his beer and then picked up the seven and replaced it with a six. Slade moved Ralph's marble back one. "Bought it from a pretty lady called Party Doll," Slade continued.

"Party Doll? Where'd you meet her?"

"She had a place on the square across from the courthouse."

"Across from the courthouse?"

"Yeah, I found her playing the game with some friends in a booth across from the bar. It was a slow day and they was all drinkin' milkshakes and she stopped long enough to fix me one."

Ralph smirked and asked, "What else did she sell you?"

"This board. She said her brother made it. Nice workmanship."

Frank questioned, "So, they played this game while they …?"

"Yeah, like I said, it was a slow day."

Monty giggled and quipped, "B-Bet th-they was g-glad to see you."

"I guess she was. She was real friendly and talkative."

"Of course she was." Ralph snickered.

"She operated right there on the square?" Frank asked.

"Yeah, between a furniture place and hardware store."

Frank shook his head. "Only in Texas. How was the … milkshake?"

"Real creamy. It was a cute place. Had an old jukebox playing Elvis songs. Had a picture of an Elvis impersonator on the wall. She said it was her son at some big event they had there to promote the business."

"Promote the business?"

"Yeah, Rock 'n Roll Soda Shoppe."

His friends busted out laughing. Slade frowned. "What's so funny?"

Stein chuckled and raised his newspaper back up. Frank tried to explain. "Well, you called her Party Doll."

Slade got it and smiled. "That was her Facebook handle."

Frank played a seven and moved his marble from the corner all the way to home. Ralph grumbled. "You know you can split that don't you?"

Monty was examining a card closely and asked, "Y-You g-get these c-cards from her too?"

"Nah, Ralph had these. My cards are pretty worn out."

Frank asked, "Where'd they come from? Looks like a most wanted list."

Ralph refilled his mouth with popcorn, played the Ace of Spades and answered, "Recognize this bum?"

As he pulled a marble out of the start box, Monty picked it up and studied it. "Oh! Th-That's Hussein, Sadamn Hussein isn't it?"

"Yeah, I got 'em when we was at war with Iraq. They're all dead now."

Slade speculated. "I guess they'll come out with Iranian thugs now."

Frank mused then added, "That would be politically incorrect these days."

Ralph farted loudly. His friends took it as his retort.

Frank looked at Slade. "Heard any more on the fugitives?"

"They fished the second one out of the Arkansas in Canon City by Veteran's Park. They think the other Cuban shot him and threw him off the train."

"Train?"

"Royal Gorge Express."

Monty's eyes lit up. "Th-That's the one Wh-White Feather's on, isn't it, Albert?"

Albert lowered his paper again and nodded. Ralph complained, "I thought you said he came back."

"We said that the train goes out through the Royal Gorge and then stops and reverses to come back through to Canon City."

Ralph cursed and took another swig of beer. Frank asked, "Why would the fugitives get on a train that goes nowhere?"

"We don't think they knew that."

Ralph loved the absurdity of it and blew beer out his nose laughing.

Frank speculated about an escape. "So he probably jumped off the train?"

"Actually, he broke into the locomotive and was forcing the engineer to head for Salida."

Frank pressed the issue. "So, are you a deputy?"

"Ex-sheriff. Sean asked me to come out here and keep an eye on the place."

Slade placed his hand on his ear. "The Cuban has been caught." He listened for a moment and then added, "Sheriff Bailey had the conductor shut down the train and they apprehended him."

Ralph looked up at the ceiling and then all around the ex-sheriff. You gettin' messages from God or something?"

Slade chuckled. "My hearing aid has blue tooth. I've got messages on the scanner feeding through it."

Ralph was even more confused. "Blue tooth? You pickin' up stuff through your teeth?"

Slade and the others burst into belly laughs. Ralph threw down his cards and stomped off.

His friends could not stop laughing. Albert cast his paper aside and intercepted his friend. "Rudolph, ignore them. You asked a perfectly logical question."

Ralph stopped but cursed under his breath.

"Blue Tooth is some weird computer thing. It connects devices to each other. Sheriff Slade has a police scanner in his pocket and uses Blue Tooth technology to connect it to his hearing aid so that he can listen to the scanner privately."

Ralph blinked rapidly as he thought about it. Frank was intrigued. "Is that how it works, Cody?"

Slade answered, "Yep."

Frank smiled. "I want one."

Slade added, "I can get my phone calls through it. I can even listen to my tunes through it."

Frank sat back and slapped his knee. "That is just too cool!"

Slade felt something tickling his ear and swatted at it hitting his knuckles against Ralph's nose. "What the ...."

Ralph cursed and then protested, "Keep still. I wanna look at this gizmo."

"It don't look any different than any other hearing aid. ... Oops, scuse me." He touched his ear piece.

"Hello." Slade listened. "Yeah, I caught it on the scanner ... yeah, okay. Thanks."

Slade looked at his curious onlookers. "Well, since they've caught him, I'm off the case. Guess I'll get packed up."

Chapter 37

Jerry Is Released

THE RIDE FROM THE Canon City Detention Center had been very quiet. Jerry and Samantha were clearly devastated. Jerry had obviously not gotten any sleep in the jail. When Samantha had seen Jerry come out from detention, she had completely broken down. So, Sam had suggested they clear up the paperwork and go somewhere to eat. He remembered that when he had last eaten at K-Bob's around this time, it was very quiet and almost empty.

He found it to be the case this time as well. There was a group of ladies playing cards in one corner and only a couple of tables occupied. Jerry chose a booth for them away from everyone. They looked over the menus and ordered before Sam started the conversation.

"So, how are you feeling, Jer?"

Jerry shrugged and kept his head down. Samantha blew her nose and sat up a little straighter. "Can you talk about it?"

Jerry glanced up at his mother, raised his shoulders and answered, "I guess."

When he did not offer more, Sam prompted him, "Can you tell us what happened? Start from the beginning."

Jerry grabbed the salt shaker and started rotating it in his fingers. "Well, we got done with the project in Alamosa really late. It was all indoor stuff, so we worked under the lights. We shut down around midnight, packed up and found an all-night diner. I fell asleep on the ride back and woke up when I heard a commotion in the truck. Jake owns a house out by the airport and there were dozens of flashing lights surrounding it."

"Silver West Airport?"

"Yeah, out south on 69. Jake started cussing and ranting and turned to go check it out. When we got there, we all stayed in the truck but Jake. He jumped out and ran up to his house. They had tape all around it and deputies and DEA were guarding the area. I couldn't hear what was being said, but Jake got animated and started pushing the deputies. They threw him to the ground and cuffed him. Then they came out and cuffed us too."

Sam huffed and turned his head in disgust. Samantha was incredulous. "Why you? You weren't doing anything."

"That's what we told 'em, but they just read us our rights and escorted us to a paddy wagon and eventually drove us to jail."

Sam and Samantha were speechless. Jerry continued, "They put us all together in a cell and Jake apologized for getting us all arrested. He told us that he just wanted to see what the renters had done to his house and got upset when they wouldn't let him go in. They told him that it was a crime scene and then started asking him what he was doing there. He told them that he was the owner of the house and was driving home with his construction crew when he had seen the lights and came over to check it out."

Jerry played with the shaker again for a moment before continuing, "Anyway, they misunderstood and accused him of being there to work on the pot."

"Work on the what?"

"You know, tend to the marijuana plants."

Samantha gasped. "Marijuana plants?"

Jerry looked up at her and then his dad. "Yeah, Jake's renters turned out to be growing marijuana in his house. Cops told him it was wall to wall throughout the house. Jake said the house would be ruined by all the water and humidity. He said that grow sites destroyed houses leaving them full of mold and rotted walls. He said it would cost a fortune to restore."

Sam shook his head. "That's what I've heard too. He may have to level it."

Jerry raised his eyebrows and nodded. Sam asked, "When did they figure out you were innocent?"

Jerry huffed. "They interrogated each of us for hours insisting that we were there to maintain the site. At some point last night they seemed to back off and then this morning we learned that they were dropping the charges. I guess Jake proved that we had been in Alamosa on a job and they finally came around to believing us."

Sam asked, "Why didn't you call me?"

Jerry shifted in his chair. "Well, we kept thinking they would figure out we were innocent. Then it got too late."

Samantha laid her hand on Jerry's wrist. "Well, it's over now. You're okay. Everything will be okay."

Sam spoke before thinking. "Did you know about the grow site?"

"Sam!" Samantha protested.

Jerry looked at his father incredulously. "No! Why would I?"

Sam held up his hands defensively. "I'm sorry. Stupid question."

He let them calm down and then proposed, "Well, as your mother says, it's over now and everything is going to be all right. Let's just eat and go home. What'dya say?"

Jerry and Samantha remained quiet. Sam's head began to spin and his heart filled with anxiety. He was certain that he had alienated his son and ex-wife with one stupid question. He shook his head and wiped his face with his hand. How would he ever recover from this?

Samantha's phone buzzed. "Tam? ... You are? ... We're at K-Bob's. ... Yes, okay."

Samantha looked at Sam and then Jerry. Tammy and David are in town. They're going to join us if that's okay?

Jerry shrugged.

|||||||||

Flambeau snapped pictures of the departing police car as Sean, Pennie and White Feather watched the Canon City police haul the Cuban off to jail. Sean looked at his watch. It was past four o'clock. He looked into Pennie's sad eyes. "What do think? Should we head up to the bridge?"

Pennie looked down and shook her head. "I just want to go home."

Sean agreed. "Yeah, let's go home."

Flambeau was now standing under a tree focusing his camera on a sparrow. White Feather was eyeing a park bench not far away. Sean felt indebted. "You fellows need a ride home?"

White Feather glanced back at Flambeau. "Much obliged."

Chapter 38

The Family at K-Bob's

Tammy Morrison rushed across the restaurant to embrace her brother Jerry. "Oh, Jerry, are you okay?"

Sam Morrison stood to greet David Ludwig, Tammy's boyfriend. "Hi, David, how's school?"

David shook Sam's hand and then shook his head, "Pretty rough semester."

Sam nodded. "Yes, I remember."

Samantha smiled and tipped her head to acknowledge David and he reciprocated. Tammy sat down beside her brother. David sat next to her. Samantha explained, "We've ordered."

Tammy grabbed the menu. "I wonder what's good?"

Sam smiled, "Well, it's K-Bob's, so probably the steak."

Samantha added, "The salad bar looks good."

Tammy threw down her menu. "Settled. It must have been dreadful, Jerry."

Jerry shrugged. "Yeah, I guess so."

"So, what happened?"

Samantha reached across the table and touched her daughter's hand. "Slow down, Tammy. Jerry needs some time."

Tammy gave her brother her pitiful face. "I'm sorry, Brother."

Jerry shrugged. "No problem. It's no big deal really. We were coming back from a job in Alamosa. We had worked well past midnight so we could get finished and come home. We got to the airport around 4:00 a.m. and saw flashing lights. The boss figured out that they were at his rental place so we drove over there. When they found out he owned the house, they arrested him and then came after us with a SWAT team."

"Oh, my God, didn't you tell them you had nothing to do with it?!"

"Of course, but they didn't believe us."

"Why'd they bring you way over here?"

"They brought all of the prisoners over here. Rockcliffe isn't big enough to handle it."

"Why didn't you call one of us?"

"Well, we were sure they were going to let us go yesterday. But, time dragged on and it was too late when we realized we weren't going to be released. I was even beginning to think we wouldn't get out today."

Tammy was incensed. "That's terrible."

The waiter came over to take the additional orders. Sam Morrison's heart was floating in air. Jerry was safe and innocent. None of his fears had been warranted. There was still the matter of Samantha's date, but everything had been like old times on the drive. And now, with the whole family together including David, he felt that maybe it would be okay.

David interrupted his thoughts. "Hey, Mrs. M, I really appreciated your help on Monday night."

Samantha gave him her motherly smile. "No problem, David. Glad I could help."

"I feel so stupid running out of gas. I haven't done that since I was sixteen."

Samantha laughed. "We've all done it. Don't worry about it."

Sam was putting the days together. Monday was the night he called Samantha to tell her about the raids. It was the night their phone call was interrupted by Tammy declaring that "He's here, Mom." It was David! David was there!

But something did not fit. "Where'd you run out of gas?"

"Dead Man's Curve. I thought maybe I could coast to town, but I forgot about the ups and downs along there. Fortunately, a good Samaritan stopped and gave me a lift in."

Sam smiled a little too broadly. "That IS fortunate. So, he took you to Samantha's?"

"Yeah, then she and Tammy took me to get gas and back out to my car."

Sam raised his glass. "Here's to good Samaritans."

Chapter 39

Goodbye Slade, Hello Metal Box

Frank carried the heavy wooden game board, Monty carried a small athletic bag, and Slade carried his suitcase. Slade's wife, Dottie, hopped out of the big Cadillac and pushed the fob to open the trunk. Slade tilted the suitcase toward Albert. "Dottie, this is Albert Stein, Monty, Ralph and Frank."

"Hidee, boys."

"Ma'am."

Slade tossed the suitcase into the trunk carelessly. Frank placed the board beside it gently. Monty set the athletic bag on top of the board. Albert reached out his hand. "It was a pleasure getting to know you, Sheriff Slade."

"You don't have to be so formal, Stein. Just call me Cody."

Albert drew back his throbbing hand as Frank offered his. "Hope to see you again one day, Cody."

Slade crushed his hand and replied, "Maybe I'll bring the board out sometime for a rematch."

Frank quipped, "Thanks to you, we've lost our marbles."

Ralph chose to pat him on the back. "Do that, Pardner."

Monty added from a distance, "It was f-fun."

They watched them drive off and then Ralph headed back toward the door to St. Jude on a mission. "Okay, let's go get it."

Frank questioned, "Get what?"

"The box, stupid."

Albert stepped in when he saw Frank clench his fists. "What box, Rudolph?"

Ralph cursed and then held out his hands. "The box, the metal box, remember?"

Monty asked, "You've g-got it?"

"It's by the dumpster."

"What dumpster?"

"By the grow site."

"By the grow site?"

"Saw it when we went over with Slade."

"Why d-didn't you g-grab it then?"

"Melton's a stickler, remember?"

Ralph led his band of old geezers straight through St. Jude and out the back door. Frank got antsy. "What if they're still there?"

"They're gone."

"How do you know?"

"I got a window, remember."

Frank shook his head in disgust and muttered, "Can't see the site from your window, stupid."

Ralph spun around and hurled a clinched fist at Frank's head. Monty grabbed his shirt by the shoulder and pulled him away. Frank assumed the boxer's pose. He was ready. He could take the stooped old geezer easy. "Remember this, stupid!" he shouted as he showed him his fists.

Ralph began windmilling and tugging against Monty's grip. Albert raised his hands. "Gentlemen, gentlemen, please stop."

As the two "gentlemen" glared at each other, Albert continued, "Save your energy for the climb over Cemetery Hill. We're all going to need it."

Frank dropped his dukes and cocked his head to one side. "Albert's right. Sorry I called you stupid but you called me stupid first."

Ralph stopped tugging and studied Frank for a moment. "Apology accepted. You're lucky I'm in a good mood today." He dropped his dukes. "Let's go."

●●●●●●●●

The old geezers were surprised to discover that Ralph had been right. The metal box sat next to the dumpster covered in miscellaneous garbage. It looked as if the Cubans had been too lazy to walk around the fence to the dumpster and were in a habit of just hurling their garbage over the Concertina wire sometimes hitting the dumpster, sometimes not.

Albert observed. "I suppose they felt that if their garbage was in the vicinity of the dumpster, the driver would pick it up."

Ralph commented, "Lucky for us, they're stupid slobs."

Frank and Monty dusted off the box and pulled it away from the garbage piles. Ralph examined the burn marks around the lid. "One more time aught to do it."

In unison, his friends replied, "Noooooo!"

Albert suggested, "I would like to get White Feather's opinion."

Ralph farted loudly as he stood. "What's an Injun know about explosives?"

Albert tried to be diplomatic by answering, "Perhaps he will think of another way."

"Crap." Ralph expressed as he headed back toward Cemetery Hill. Frank and Monty looked at each other. Frank reminded him. "I carried it up the hill last time."

Monty moaned and then the big man hoisted the box up onto his shoulder.

▓▓▓▓▓▓▓

After dinner, White Feather examined the scorched metal around the lid. Ralph proclaimed, "One more time will do it."

White Feather looked at Ralph incredulously. "I'll take it in to Cal tomorrow."

"Who's Cal?"

"Welder. Will cut it open." White Feather pulled out his cell phone and called to schedule a ride on the Rotary Van.

"Why don't you just buy a car?" Frank joked.

Ralph added, "How about an Injun motorcycle." He found his little joke hilarious.

Frank warned, "You're gonna get scalped one of these days and we're not gonna help you."

Ralph drew back his fist but Monty grabbed his wrist. Frank held up his hands. "Sorry, Ralph, just jokin' with you."

Ralph was slow to cool down. Monty became the peacemaker. "L-Let's g-go p-play pool."

It worked. "You and me against the Injun and stupid."

Albert jumped in. "Rudolph! That was uncalled for."

Frank patted Albert on the shoulder. "It's okay, Albert, sticks and stones. Besides, twinkle, twinkle little star, what you say is what you are."

Albert shook his head. "Are you two in grade school?"

Ralph turned to charge Frank when White Feather ducked to plant his shoulder in Ralph's stomach, then stood up and carried him kicking and flailing to the pool room surrounded by howls of laughter.

PART IV:

Life Goes On

Chapter 40

Box Opened, Frank Thwarted

THE LARGE METAL BUILDING was lit up like Christmas by the flashing lights of the deputies' vehicles. Sheriff Bailey stood by as Deputy Morrison questioned the Sleuthkateers about the skeleton found in the metal box. Al Vanderburg, the coroner, rushed in. "Hey, Al," Bailey greeted."

"Hey, Sean, what've we got?"

"The guys," he nodded toward the Sleuthkateers, "found a metal box buried in the St. Jude catacombs. When Cal cut it open they found a skeleton in it. Looks like a baby or fetus, maybe."

Al examined the box and then brushed Morrison aside. "What do you know about this?"

Morrison countered, "They were just telling me that they think it is the aborted baby of Joyce Rommel."

"Sounds familiar."

"She's the lady who stabbed a lady years ago and then came back and stabbed Elizabeth Dawson."

"Oh, yes, I remember now. Aborted baby, eh?"

"Stein tells me that Joyce's baby was aborted in St. Jude back when it was an Institution for the Insane. Supposedly, Rommel was looking for the fetus when Elizabeth surprised her. So, Albert and the gang dug up the box and brought it to Cal to open."

Al turned to the sheriff. "I'm gonna need to get in touch with Rommel."

Sean nodded. "I'll have Buster set it up."

"Okay, I'll take the box now," said the coroner."

"Absolutely, please do!" Cal replied. "I don't want that spooky thing around here."

⊥⊥⊥⊥⊥⊥⊥⊥⊥

On the ride back to St. Jude from Cal's Welding Shop, Frank's mind wandered back to his boorish rebuke of poor Trudy. The thought made him shudder. He was not like that. He saw himself as a kind man, not a cruel, self-centered, arrogant male chauvinist. He made a promise to himself that as soon as they returned, he would go straight to Trudy and try to smooth things over. He had faith in his charm and his ability to turn around his indiscretion and make things right with her. He began to fantasize about what a closer relationship with the delightful lady might be like.

The Rotary Van rocked side to side as it turned off Highway 69 onto the road up to St. Jude. Frank gripped the seat in front of him and tried to force himself to rehearse his meeting with Trudy.

By the time the van pulled up to the front door, Frank felt ready and he was eager to go in to find her. But as Frank entered the reception area, Nurse Nugent was waiting for him. She frowned and pointed her pointing finger at him and wiggled it demanding he come to her immediately! He did.

"I understand you have one of Benjamin Cook's canisters! They were supposed to have been confiscated after Benny's poisoning. Cough it up!"

Frank gasped. "I don't have one of those."

"You admitted it to Trudy, didn't you?"

"I was just joking about that. I don't ...."

"I don't want to hear it. Cough it up."

His friends gathered around to witness his dressing down. Ralph was miffed. "Where'd you get more canisters?"

"Ralph! I don't have one. They were all turned in."

Nugent questioned, "Did you or did you not tell Trudy that you had one?"

"Again, I was joking," Frank reiterated. "It was a bad joke. I regret it. I wish I hadn't said it. I want to apologize to her."

Ralph butted in, saying, "You should apologize to us."

Albert tapped Ralph on his shoulder. "Let's move along, Rudolph. Frank denies having the potion. It's none of our business."

Ralph brushed Albert's hand off his shoulder. "It's not fair."

White Feather grabbed the back of his collar and moved him along. "You have no use for love potion."

Ralph was waving his arms trying to free himself. "Well, oh yeah?"

"Come to me. I fix."

Nugent ignored the side show. "All right, then, you give me no choice. We will search your room."

"Fine. Go ahead. You won't find anything."

"Oh, really? Where did you hide it?"

"I didn't hide it because I don't have it."

Nugent spun around and stormed off. Frank followed her up to his room but was made to remain in the hallway while she ransacked his room.

Word got out quickly and residents began to accumulate to watch the spectacle. Frank wondered how angry Nurse Nugent would be if she found something because she was furious not finding anything.

||||||||||

All eyes were on Frank as he entered the dining room. He was late for lunch because he wanted to get his room back to some semblance of order after Nugent had finally given up on her campaign to find what did not exist. The focus on him made him block out the world and go straight to get his food tray and drink and make a beeline to his table. Albert asked, "You okay, Franklin?"

Frank shrugged. "The room is almost back to usable."

Ralph gave his advice. "The Injun can fix you up."

"Fix me up?"

"Yeah. Love potions. He makes 'em."

Even White Feather found that laughable. It broke the ice and the old geezers relaxed.

Frank sneaked a peek at Trudy's table. Her back was to him, but he noticed that Ruth was giving him the evil eye. Why would Ruth be upset with him.

Then he began to think of a myriad of reasons why Ruth might be upset with him. The most obvious reason might be because she had heard what he had said to Trudy. If there was one thing you could depend upon it was that the ladies shared everything. Then there was the fact that he had almost ignored her since that day they had shared tea in her room and talked about Lizzie. He had felt that they had become very close that day. Perhaps, she had felt it too. But because he had hardly spoken to her since then, maybe she was upset about that.

Frank shook his head. It was not his fault. He was eighty-seven going on eighty-eight. It was not like he was an eligible bachelor. He shook his head again. But then again ... in this place, he was an eligible bachelor. In fact, in his modest opinion, the best catch in the Home.

He looked up and his friends were smiling at him. Ralph explained it to him. "You havin' a seizure?"

Frank frowned and retorted, "What're you talkin' about?"

Ralph started shaking his head spastically as if imitating him. The others snickered. Albert interceded, "We just noticed, Franklin, that you are shaking your head a lot. What are you conflicted about? Are you still upset about Nurse Nugent?"

Frank chuckled and shook his head again. Ralph pointed and remarked, "Yeah, like that."

Frank raised his eyebrows and tilted his head to one side. "No, it's not about Nugent."

"Care to share?"

"Well, it's personal."

Ralph stuffed his mouth with peas and asked, "Personal? Around here?"

White Feather folded his arms, closed his eyes and muttered, "Girl problems."

His friends looked stunned and confused. Frank was indignant. "How'd you know ..." he caught himself saying, but it was too late.

Albert studied him. "Is it true, Franklin? Are you having trouble with the ladies? So, what IS happening between you and Trudy?"

Monty swelled up with bug eyes and oval mouth as if discovering a secret.

Ralph was lost. "Trudy?" He glanced at the ladies' table. "That hag?"

Frank wanted to slug Ralph for being so inconsiderate. But, of course, that would really show his weakness for her. He held out his hands apologetically. "It's just that I said some things I shouldn't have and I regret it."

Monty was about to burst. "Wh-What d-did you s-say?"

"Where do I begin? It was haircut day. I hate haircut day. The ladies all feel so pretty and flirty. Plus, I don't like to get my hair cut in a SALON."

Ralph agreed with that. "Me either. We need a barber shop."

White Feather pulled out his Bowie-style knife. "Open for business."

Frank raised his hands in defense. "I hope you are kidding."

Albert tried to get them back on track. "So, what happened, Franklin?"

"Oh. Well, Trudy came waltzing up to me all flirty and everything and I just kind of snapped."

"What did you say?"

"I told her I had some of Benny's potion left over. Would she want to come up after dinner."

His friends hoorayed him and folded over in laughter. Frank noticed that they were drawing the attention of the ladies' table. He prayed they had not heard him. The ladies began shaking their heads and whispering among themselves with angry eyes. Frank wanted to crawl under the table.

He saw any chance of ever reconciling with Trudy or Ruth slipping away.

Chapter 41

On the Bench Again

Frank NOTICED IT THE minute he walked out the back door of St. Jude. One of the old ladies was sitting on his bench. He approached the bench with disdain, but began to change his mood as he got closer and recognized Trudy sitting quietly admiring the colors in the pond.

"Miss Trudy," he declared with a broad sweeping bow.

She giggled and replied, "Mr. Franklin."

"May I join you?"

"If you must."

"Oh, yes, I must. I owe you the most heartfelt apology. I was a dreadful cad the other day and I regret it deeply."

Trudy shifted and avoided looking at him. "Yes you were. Please, sit down."

Frank sat beside her at a respectable distance. "The pond is colorful this evening. So pretty ... like you."

"Pssst. Enough of that gibberish. I forgive you, already."

Frank exhaled noisily as if her forgiveness was such a relief.

They sat in silence for a while. When Frank noticed that Trudy was looking at the crooked old juniper, he asked, "Do you believe in time travel?"

"Oh, yes, I love that show."

Frank was taken aback. "Show? What show?"

"Oh, well *Outlander*. We've been watching it on Netflix."

"*Outlander,* eh? I haven't seen it. Is it good?"

"Yes! It is an amazing series. We just love it."

Frank paused for a moment and then asked, "If you could go back in time, to what point would you return?"

"Late eighteenth century, I think."

Again Frank was thrown off. "That's curious. Why then?"

Trudy's face lit up. "I would love to meet Jane Austen. I just love her novels."

Frank was becoming flummoxed. "I don't think I've read any of them. What are they about?"

Trudy looked at him as if appalled. "*Pride and Prejudice? Sense and Sensibility?*"

"I've heard of them, just never read them."

"It was required reading when I went to school."

"Hmmm. I don't think they were out yet when I went to school."

Trudy slapped his knee and giggled. "Oh, silly, you're not THAT old."

Frank smiled. "Just feels like it sometimes."

Trudy was silent. Frank tried again. "What if you had to go back to some point in your life? What point would that be?"

Trudy thought about it and then shook her head. "I don't want to go back." She began to sob. "I don't want to relive Stan's death."

Frank could completely empathize with her. "I'm sorry, Trudy. And I wouldn't want to go through my wife and daughter's accident again."

She glanced at him as she pulled a tissue from her purse. "What happened?"

Frank felt his eyes tearing up. "Automobile accident. What happened to Stan?"

"Cancer."

Frank extracted his handkerchief from his hip pocket and dried his eyes. "I didn't think about that aspect, Trudy. Reliving all the deaths over the years... grandparents, parents, siblings, friends."

Trudy blew her nose. "It's amazing we have a heart left."

"It should be hard as a rock, but it feels raw. Like dozens of open wounds."

Trudy turned to hug him and he reached out to embrace her. They sobbed uncontrollably for several tender moments. That settled it. He would tell White Feather that he was not interested in time travel. He would respectfully ask him to stop talking about it.

They released each other and Trudy dug in her purse for another tissue. "What brought up that dreary subject?"

Frank opened his mouth but then restrained himself. White Feather's time travel scheme seemed trivial and childish at this moment. What could his motive be? White Feather was too cerebral, too wise for such nonsense. Suddenly, White Feather's intentions became very suspect. What was the old medicine man really up to? Was it just one of his elaborate practical jokes or some deep mystical side of him? Trudy was waiting for an answer.

"I apologize, Trudy. It was just a silly discussion I had with White Feather. I didn't intend for it to stir up sad memories."

Trudy shook her head. "I'm sorry, Frank. I didn't intend to get morbid on you."

"No, you answered my question honestly and sincerely. I respect you for that. And I apologize if I hurt you."

"Not your fault. I haven't talked about Stan in a long time." She looked at him with hopeful eyes, glistening from the tears.

She touched his heart. "I feel deeply honored that you feel you can open up to me." He shifted uncomfortably. "At least I hope you feel that way."

Trudy reached for his hand. "You're a nice man, Frank." Then her optimistic and playful personality kicked in. "I don't care what they all say."

They enjoyed a good consoling laugh.

Trudy shivered. Frank asked, "Are you chilled? Should we go inside?"

She pulled her shawl tight around her. "How about a walk? Ruth tells me there is a nice trail that goes through the trees to the southern side of the property. Have you walked it?"

"First I've heard of it. You know where it starts?"

Trudy rolled her eyes. "No idea. I've declined Ruth's invitations. I'm not the outdoorsy type."

They laughed. Frank stood and proposed, "Let's go explore a new path."

As Trudy took his hand and stood to join him, Frank's eyes glimpsed a shadow behind the back door of St. Jude. "Ruth?"

Chapter 42

A Columbine Flower and a Dark Sky

THE COLUMBINE LADIES BEGAN to congregate in the old familiar community room at the library. The conversation was already abuzz about their adventure on the Royal Gorge Express.

Florence bragged, "I saw the murderer, you know."

"You SAW him?"

"Yes, on the observation deck. I could tell by the look in his eye that he was up to no good."

"No you couldn't!"

"I told the sheriff and he admitted that he was the guy."

"No he didn't!"

"Yes, he did."

Maybell joined in. "Sheriff shot him with my pistol."

"He didn't shoot him."

"If it hadn't been for my gun, he'd have got away."

"I couldn't believe you jumped into the Arkansas off that bridge, Maybell. That was crazy!"

"And then Bessie jumped in. Lordy, what craziness."

Lena called the meeting to order. "Ladies ... ladies, please. ... Thank you. I know we are all anxious to rehash our ..." she fashioned quote marks with her fingers, "'adventure' on the train, but I would like to take care of a little business if we could. I think we should consider asking Pennie to join us as an alternate."

Florence raised her hand and waved it enthusiastically. Lena recognized her. "I make a motion that we induct Pennie Bailey into our club!"

Elizabeth shouted out, "I second."

Lena repeated the motion adding, "… as an alternate. Show of hands?"

It was unanimous.

Then quiet, thoughtful Theresa surprised everyone by raising her hand. Lena recognized her. "I think we should send a Columbine to Sheriff Bailey and that nice Mr. White Feather."

Maybell stood up and waved her pistol. "Not that murderin' Injun."

Lena shook her head. "Maybell, if you don't put that dreadful gun away, I will confiscate it myself and return it to the sheriff."

Bessie shouted at Maybell. "He helped find the murderer. You were wrong about him the whole time."

Maybell was livid. "Oh, sure he's got all of you bamboozled along with the sheriff, but I say he ain't nothin' but a thievin' Injun."

An anonymous voice declared, "Would somebody shoot her!"

Laughter and hoots seized the members. Even Lena had to break for a giggle.

Lena waved her arms to restore order. "We have a motion to send Columbines to Sheriff Bailey and 'that nice Mr. White Feather.' Is there a second?"

Twenty-two of the twenty-four members shouted, "I second."

Maybell waved her hand as if totally disgusted with the whole bunch.

"All in favor?"

Twenty-two hands went up plus President Lena's. Then, to everyone's surprise, Maybell reluctantly raised hers as well.

"Apposed?"

There were none.

Lena could not resist asking, "Why did you raise your hand in favor, Maybell?"

"Well ... yeah, he's kinda cute, I guess."

And that brought the house down.

After the meeting, as Lena reached to turn out the lights, she noticed that someone had placed a framed picture of "that nice Mr. White Feather" on the Columbine bulletin board.

🚊

White Feather sat on a park bench on the west side of Bluff Park admiring the sun paint the clouds a fiery red, intense orange framed by soft blues as it descended behind the Sangre de Cristo Mountain Range. He whispered an ancient chant blessing the valley and the living things and asking the white raven to bring peace.

Nearby a couple carrying tote bags approached a rustic looking twelve-foot square shed covered by a brown metal roof. They unlocked the door on the east side and entered. After a few minutes, the roof of the old shed began to roll back revealing a room lined with benches on the south and north side; a computer on a shelf beside a large flat screen TV on the west side; and something huge mounted on a pedestal in the center covered by a silver shroud.

White Feather scanned the sky. Only the ancestor camp fires named Jupiter and Saturn were visible in the twilight. Soon there would be others. Inside the shed, the man pulled off the shroud revealing a large telescope as the woman fired up the computer. They worked quietly with the expertise that comes with having done something many times. The woman remarked, "Going to Home."

Suddenly, the telescope began to buzz and move in a slow arcing motion before stopping pointed southwest at an angle. The man pulled what looked like several small flashlights out of the tote. He hung one over his neck, stuck something in his pocket and handed something to the woman. He then pulled out a clipboard, scanned it and declared, "Let's point it at Jupiter to get started."

The woman typed something into the computer and the barrel-shaped telescope began to move again in a slow swooping arc until it was pointing at the brightest light in the sky. White Feather was amused by the grinding whir of the gears and the graceful movement of the big scope.

Cars pulled into the parking lot on the east side of Bluff Park. The woman in the observatory commented, "Sounds like our guests are arriving."

The man stepped up on the bench on the north side to peer out. "Yep, looks like they're here. I'll go escort them down."

The man headed for the parking lot. The woman kept herself busy setting up things.

When the man came back he was followed by ten people including several kids. As they filled the little observatory and made their introductions, White Feather made note that the star guides were named Don and Kay.

The party found seats and Don pulled up an adjustable astronomer's chair. He began his presentation with, "The Smokey Jack Observatory was named after Suzanne Jack who was a prominent rancher in the valley. She watched the light domes from Colorado Springs and Pueblo growing ever brighter and worried that her grandchildren might not be able to see the Milky Way someday. So, she formed the Dark Skies group and their mission was, and still is, to preserve the dark skies of this beautiful valley for future generations. Our solution is simple, really. It is to put hoods on all of the lights in the valley so that the light shines down where the light is needed but not up into the sky where it is wasted and where the glare bleaches out the darkness. In 2015, the International Dark Skies Association certified Rockcliffe as a Dark Sky Community. In honor of the certification, local businesses donated the materials and volunteers built this observatory."

He paused to give the visitors a moment to look up at the darkening sky where the constellations were beginning to appear and the glow of the sun was all but extinguished in the west behind the mountains.

"The Smokey Jack Observatory is not a traditional domed observatory. It is what the astronomers call a 'roll off' observatory. It is often the preferred style chosen by amateur astronomers. As you can see, it looks like a regular twelve-foot square shed except that the roof rolls back to open it up to the night sky. The walls on the north and south are only about chest high opening up the southern and northern skies fully for observation. The telescope is a 14-inch Schmidt-Cassegrain. That means that light comes in from the front, bounces off mirrors in the back, reflecting off mirrors in the front sending light back through the rear into the lens. This configuration enables the scope to have a nice compact design while still giving us a long focal length."

Someone commented, "Is everything in Colorado a fourteener?"

Everyone laughed. Don commented, "What he is referring to is that there are fifty-eight fourteeners in Colorado."

"What's a fourteener?"

"It's a peak that is a minimum of fourteen thousand feet high. So, naturally we would want our telescope to be fourteen inches, wouldn't we?"

Don pointed to his wife. "Kay is our Telescope Navigation Engineer."

Kay appeared to be embarrassed. "Oh, I'm no engineer. I just type in the object and the software tells the telescope where to point."

Don looked up. "Well, the constellations are starting to come out." He pulled out a device a little larger than a fat sharpie and clicked on an extremely bright green laser to point out the Big Dipper and the North Star, Polaris. Then he pointed it across the sky from the southeast to northeast. "The Milky Way is starting to appear."

There was a collective "Awe."

A woman screamed. Everyone jerked their heads around to see the faint shadow of White Feather standing silently just outside the observatory looking in.

"We call it Cornmeal Trail," said White Feather.

The stunned group tried to understand what they were seeing. Don could feel his heart racing. "Sir, are you here for the star party?"

"I saw add for star guide."

"Are you volunteering as a star guide?"

"I know Indian version."

"Great!" Don walked across to shake his hand. "I am Don and that is Kay."

"White Feather."

Don asked, "Would you like to come in and give us the Native American version of the night sky?"

"I stand here."

"Do you have a Milky Way story, White Feather?"

White Feather folded his arms and closed his eyes. "I will tell the story I heard from the elders when I was a boy. The women had ground corn and stored the cornmeal in huts. They noticed that the level dropped overnight so they stayed up to see who was stealing the meal. At midnight, they looked in and saw a mystical wolf standing knee deep and lapping up the delicious meal. They shouted and waved sticks and the wolf bolted out of the hut and raced across the sky leaving a trail of cornmeal."

One of the visitors remarked, "What a wonderful story."

Don looked at Kay and raised his eyebrows and smiled. "Shall we take a look at some constellations?"

White Feather volunteered. "Campfires of the ancestors."

"Constellations?"

"Stars."

"How about the Pleiades? Did your ancestors call it seven sisters?"

"Ani'tsutsa, The Disrespectful Boys."

"Great, White Feather, please tell that story ...."

White Feather looked up at the sky to begin his story, while in the darkness, another story was unfolding.

Lunch with the Columbine Club. Front row from left: Judy Keyes, Jacke Barnes, Joanie Liebman. Second row from left: Judy Papantonis, June Kilbourn, Virginia Kness, Addie Heck, Paulie Canda, Barb Eberling. Third row from left: Patty Pickerill, Anne Marie Donahoe, Pat Gibson, Judy Lynch, Mary Horton, Linda Tyler, Sandy Dunlap, Doris Porth, Kathy Boulee, Myrtle Schulze, Gayle Bradburn, Nancy North, Gail Frickell, Phyllis Dearborn, Monte Hess, Carol Vimont
– Trib photo by Tracy Ballard

Happy 100th Anniversary to Valley's Venerable Ccolumbine Organization

COLUMBINE CLUB, YOU DON'T look a day over 50! Members of the Custer County Columbine Club gathered to reminisce and celebrate their club's 100th birthday on Thursday, May 3, 2018.

The Columbine Club was established in April of 1918 at the home of Mrs. William Griffin at the request of Mrs. Bert A. Nelson. They intended the club to be a community service and social organization.

Much has changed in the years since its creation, but two things have remained the same: they never have any more or any fewer than 24 members, and they meet on the same day each month, that is the first Tuesday.

Sadly, the names of the 24 original ladies in the club are unknown. They also only have copies of minutes from January 1976 through the present.

As was true in many clubs and organizations, when there was a "vacancy," members encouraged their daughters, sisters, or other female family members to apply.

The Columbine Club has been in service to the community in many ways in the last century to present time. Before the new school was completed in 1924, members held a "curtain carnival," which gave the $383 so they could buy and have installed stage curtains. During that same time, they bought 22 chairs for the auditorium. The club also bought a box of cigars to be presented to Mr. Doyle, "for an article in the *Wet Mountain Tribune*." They have held carnivals, bake sales, and other activities to give items to the less fortunate, donated to cancer drives, and recently, they donated to the health fair and to VALI Assisted Living.

In the club's constitution, refreshments were always limited to two types of food and drinks. In minutes taken in September 1977, secretary Ginny Kness stated that "Cream puffs with chocolate filling were enjoyed by all— minus the calories." Refreshments were always served on china, including teacups and flatware. If one was the hostess for said month, she was also responsible for table favors for each guest.

In the 1950s, the Club began meeting in the Community Room on Main Street, Westcliffe, and occasionally met in alternative places. For example, in fall of 1984, the Columbine Club met at the Rainbow Room, which we now know as the dance studio across from Custer County School, when the

West Custer County Library was holding a craft fair at the time. In mid-2003, they sold the Community Room to the library for $1.00. They asked that the room be named after Dorothea Tinkham, in honor of the lady that gave the building to the community.

Present members were treated to an elegant luncheon complete with lovely salads, chocolate covered strawberries, and a birthday cake, of course! All served beautifully on fine china. Paulie Canda said it all when she frequently exclaimed, "Isn't this so lovely?!"

The Columbine Club has a very interesting and rich history. Its members have served our community, played cards and sipped tea, and formed a strong sisterhood that few have been privy to. Happy Birthday, ladies! Here's to your next 100.

—Tracy Ballard

In honor of the 100th anniversary of the Wet Mountain Valley
Columbine Club, member Jacke Barnes put together
a history of the club for a presentation to the club members.
What follows is a transcript of that presentation:

Columbine History by Jacke Barnes

As you can guess, trying to condense 100 years of history into a "relatively" short talk is nearly impossible. We are fortunate to have minutes from January 1976 to the present. These minutes were a tremendous help in compiling this brief history. As with minutes of any group, the minutes reflect the personality of the Secretary, some minutes were extensive and for a few years in the mid-'90s the minutes could only be called minimal—very minimal.

Columbine Club was organized in April 1918 at the home of Mrs. William [Orlena—Lena] Griffin at the suggestion of Mrs. Griffin and Mrs. Bert A. [Bessie] Nelson as a community service and social organization. Although several things have changed for the Club over the years, two items in the constitution that have not changed are the number of members — 24— and the day of the meeting—the first Tuesday of each month.

In the constitution, Columbine Club's additional purposes were listed as sociability, charity, civic improvement and needlework. One could speculate that the ladies who gathered together to sew and roll bandages and knit socks during World War I so enjoyed these social and work parties that the organization of Columbine was a natural progression from those gatherings.

Charter members of the Columbine were "farm women" from the Ula area. It is unfortunate we do not know the names of the 24 originating members. And, equally unfortunate we do not have minutes of their meetings from those early years. From the quilt, which we believe commemorated the 50th anniversary of Columbine, and from the 1920 census, additional names of probable organizing ladies are: Theresa C. Stewart, Elizabeth Mercier, Betsie Callaghan, Mary [or Maybell] Haskell, and Florence Wright.

Appointed committees for Columbine were: the Membership Committee who sent invitations to those [who] have been voted to be desirable members of the Club; the Flower Committee who ordered flowers for sick or deceased members; and the Charity Committee who reported on charity cases and purchased necessary articles approved by the club.

As with any other organization, the members encouraged their daughters, sisters or other relatives, to join the club as vacancies occurred. An early member of Columbine Club was Lucy Lillie DeWall, sister to Bessie Lillie Nelson. Lucy joined the Club in 1921 at age 17. An article and photo in the Canon City Daily record in February 1980 listed Lucy Lillie DeWall as Columbine's oldest member. In 1983 Lucy resigned as a member and moved to Canon City.

Original meetings were in the homes of the members. An article in the 1921 *Wet Mountain Tribune* reporting on the September meeting stated as roll was called, each member responded with a short quotation by some of our famous men. And following the roll call, several members were asked to relate stories of the younger days. In addition,

Mrs. Napoleon Mercier, "who possesses a very sweet voice," entertained the ladies with a beautiful solo. Then a long business meeting was held, the primary discussion point was when the ladies would entertain their husbands and families.

Columbine Club has served the community in many ways throughout the years. Prior to the completion of the new school in 1924, club members held a Curtain Carnival, which netted $383 for the purchase and installation of stage curtains; they also purchased 22 chairs for the auditorium at that time. And, the Club purchased a box of cigars to be given to Mr. Doyle for an article published in the *Tribune*. Club members held carnivals, bake sales and other activities to supply baskets of food and clothing for the needy, donated to cancer drives, and in more recent years Columbine has donated to the Health Fair and to VALI.

Notes from March 1954 included a motion to cash in bonds to donate $50.00 for new stage curtains for the high school, and pies were donated to the Health Committee dance to help pay remaining indebtedness on the doctor's office. Members saved Folger Stars for another coffee maker and Genevieve Stewart collected cards, records, books, etc., from members for Fort Carson. Over the years donations were given to the Reading Is Fundamental program and to a boys ranch in the Denver area.

After years of meeting in the homes of members, the gift of the building by Mrs. Dorthea Tinkham for use by various organizations was gratefully accepted and the Civic Association was formed. The Civic Association members were comprised of Columbine Club, The Chamber of Commerce, Saddle Club, Women's Club, Rotary and the Library. The Civic

Association assessed each organization a specific amount for the use of the room. In 1956 a member paid 10 cents a month in dues and at the end of the year members paid $2.00 each to cover the $48.00 due to the Civic Association. By 1989, the assessment was $3.00 per member for a total of $72.00 per year; in 1994 the assessment was $150.00 per year.

As a member of the Civic Association and being partly responsible for the upkeep of the Community Building, many of the minutes reflected a variety of needed repairs or items for the building: 1976, the building needed a new broom; in 1979 new light fixtures were purchased by cashing in two $25 bonds; in 1981 it was determined the sweeper should be retired. It took several months of discussion before one supposes the new sweeper was purchased. In 1983 there was a shortage of flatware and Columbine Club purchased 24 place settings of inexpensive flatware. The next month the decision was made that the new flatware would not be left in the building, rather the next hostess would take the flatware home with her. In July 1983, paint was purchased for the wainscoting and wood trim in the main room. The kitchen was painted in 1988, and funding from Columbine completed that project. Other projects funded by Columbine were: a ceiling fan; building of storage units [Addie and Carl Heck]; adding mini-blinds and other window coverings; and storm doors.

As many of you know, the current Community Building started out as an apartment with bedrooms in the rear, a kitchen and the meeting place at the front of the building. The Civic Association rented the apartment out for several years. The rental agreement of 1990 between the Civic

Association and the tenant was for $100 per month rent. The tenant was responsible for all the utilities and was also tasked with the following:

1. To unlock all doors for public use by 8 a.m. every day
2. To be sure all doors are locked after any public gathering and set the thermostat at 65 degrees
3. To be appropriately dressed whenever leaving the apartment
4. To not attend any private meeting unless invited
5. To keep no household pets without written consent
6. To keep apartment, kitchen and community room clean and sanitary

After the Community Room became available there were few occasions when the Club met in alternative places. In the fall of 1984 Columbine met at the Rainbow Room since the Library was holding a craft fair in the Community Room. After much research, it was determined the Rainbow Room is the building across from the school currently the dance studio. Starting in the fall of 1989, members met in homes during a remodel of the Community Room.

In November 2002 it was with great relief that the Library assumed responsibility of the Community Room from the Civic Association, this included scheduling the building for rent and more importantly not having to deal with the continuing maintenance issues of the building. In mid-2003 the Civic Association sold the Community Room to the Library for $1.00.

In mid-2004 the Library decided to replace the building. Columbine Club then met at the Senior Center in Silver Cliff. It was at this time the members decided to scale back on refreshments and the use of China and flatware for meetings. The new building was started in August 2004 and completed in June 2005. Although still known as the Community Room, the Civic Association asked that the room be named the Dorothea Tinkham Community Room in honor of the lady who gave the building to the citizens of the county.

In the constitution, refreshments for the club were limited to two kinds of food and drinks. In September 1977, acting secretary Ginny Kness noted that cream puffs with chocolate filling were enjoyed by all--minus all the calories. Depending on the secretary, information about served refreshments and decorations varied from a simple statement to an extensive description of how the table was decorated and what refreshments were served. Refreshments were always served on China, with teacups and flatware. The only paper product used was napkins.

During this time, as hostess you were also to bring table favors for each member. Man oh man, it was sometimes a real challenge. Oriental Trading Company wasn't as readily available. Finding 24 cute favors sometimes proved difficult. These favors varied from small gift baskets with violets [courtesy of Ginny Kness], to small ceramic trees and eggshell Santas. One certainly wishes the Secretary had expanded on her description of "egg shell" Santas.

In early December, Columbine Club was responsible for decorating the Christmas tree for the enjoyment of all who rented the Community Building. In the minutes of several December meetings, there was discussion about the Christmas tree usually concerning the purchase of a new tree—on sale—after the holidays. And at one point, it was decided new lights were needed because the old lights were scorching the branches. Some of us will remember the last Christmas tree. The artificial tree had long lost any of the instructions for setting it up; color coded wire "stems" for the branches were to be matched and inserted in the color coded trunk. No matter how hard one tried, the tree resembled Charlie Brown's famous Christmas tree. Most of us were delighted when we moved out of the Community Room during the remodel and the tree was discarded.

Traditionally we exchange gifts at the December meeting. After becoming a member in the Civic Association, there were many years the members would donate $2.00, or the amount of an exchange gift, to the Association for the upkeep of the building.

Minutes of most meetings reflected health concerns and, unfortunately, the passing of many members. In the early years $5.00 was sent to any member hospitalized overnight. That amount was increased to $10.00 and finally discontinued. When a long-time member passed, a memorial was donated to an organization, or in many cases a book was donated to the library. We continue to honor our honorary members with the purchase of plants at Christmas time.

Other items of interest in the minutes: The club participated in the 4th of July parade in 1984, winning 3rd place for its float depicting a centennial theme. For the centennial of the town, members created bonnets for themselves and also had bonnets for sale at Evie's. The August 1988 minutes included the following statement: "that the Sheriff's Department would not issue parking tickets on Thursdays as several clubs meet in this building on that day.

As I said in the beginning, condensing 100 years of history into a short talk is nearly impossible. Several long-time members—Ginny Kness, Addie Heck, Paulie Canda, Barb Eberling, Judy Papantonis and Linda Tyle—can certainly add insight and comments to this history.

The Marijuana Story

Colorado Governor John Hickenlooper officially signed the Colorado Amendment 64 on Monday, December 10, 2012. This controversial ballot measure amended the Constitution of the State of Colorado outlining a statewide drug policy for cannabis making private consumption of marijuana legal in Colorado.

Shortly after its passing Hickenlooper stated, "This will be a complicated process, but we intend to follow through. That said, federal law still says marijuana is an illegal drug, so don't break out the Cheetos and Goldfish too quickly."

Although Colorado voters approved the constitutional amendment legalizing retail sales of marijuana for recreational purposes, the amendment and enabling legislation also provided that localities could limit or ban retail outlets within a city or unincorporated portion of a county through a "local option."

Custer County voted against retail sales and production of marijuana. However, the rural nature of Custer County provided a cover for illegal grow sites to pop up in the forests and in some of the large residential homes.

The September 3, 2015, edition of the *Wet Mountain Tribune* reported:

> Eight illegal marijuana grow facilities were raided in pre-dawn hours Tuesday, September 1, in Custer and Fremont Counties and at least four arrests were made.
>
> The bust was coordinated by the U.S. Attorney General's Office and run by the Drug Enforcement

Administration (DEA) out of Denver. Close to 100 law enforcement officers from at least seven local, regional, state and federal agencies were involved in the busts, which got underway at 3 a.m. Tuesday.

Summary of the game of Court Whist

Coronation
Total tricks taken to be scored
Holder King of Spades (Calls Trumps)
Holder King of Clubs (Calls Trumps)
Holder Queen of Hearts (Calls Trumps)
Holder Queen of Diamonds (Calls Trumps)

Prosperity
Each trick counts double
Spades are Trumps
Hearts are Trumps
Clubs are Trumps
Diamonds are Trumps

Conspiracy
No partners, score individually
Cut for Trumps
Cut for Trumps
Cut for Trumps
Cut for Trumps

Revolution
Each side scores opponents tricks
No Trumps
No Trumps
No Trumps
No Trumps

Confiscation
Speak after cards are dealt, lose 3 points
Spades are Trumps
Hearts are Trumps
Clubs are Trumps
Diamonds are Trumps

Restoration
Additionally count the four honors
Spades are Trumps
Hearts are Trumps
Clubs are Trumps
Diamonds are Trumps

About the Author

Courtney Miller is the multi-award winning author of the seven-book series, *The Cherokee Chronicles*. He is considered an expert on ancient Native American culture and incorporates that knowledge into his writing. He has written over 200 articles on the art, archaeology, astronomy, history and culture of ancient Native America for Native American Antiquity and other online ezines. *The Cherokee Chronicles* has received multiple awards including the CAL Literary Award for Literary Novel (*Gihli, The Chief Named Dog*) and widespread praise from the Cherokee community for authenticity.

In the White Feather Mysteries, Miller once again shows his award-winning talent for story telling bringing to life fresh characters with twisting plots and surprise endings. Miller has enjoyed entering the genre of "Geezer Lit" defining the new genre as "written about old geezers, by an old geezer."

Courtney lives with his wife, Lin, in the Wet Mountain Valley of Colorado where the White Feather Mysteries are set. He enjoys playing golf, is active in the local Rotary Club,

Friends of Beckwith Ranch, and volunteers as a star guide for the Smokey Jack Observatory.

Learn more about Courtney and his writing at the website: **www.CourtneyMillerAuthor.com**

Courtney Miller's White Feather Mystery Series: Get them all!